Bolan crouched near the door and peered through the keyhole

He knew at once that the man wearing two-tone shoes, a cream shantung suit and the thermonuclear smile was Jacques Edouard Treynet.

In front of him four youths were lolling in leather armchairs: one was a huge, fleshy hulk whose vacant eyes suggested stunted intelligence; two were rat-faced punks with greasy hair; and the fourth, a thin wiry youth, looked the most dangerous.

"This snooper," Treynet was saying, "must not be allowed to leave the property. He has to be eliminated. Is that clear, Bonzo?"

"We'll take care of him," the thin boy replied.

Then the giant spoke. "Maybe you would let me work him over? Please?" His tone was wheedling.

"Patience, Moon," Bonzo soothed. "You can have him for the last rites, okay?"

Bolan whirled as a hand suddenly touched his shoulder and a voice whispered in his ear.

"You do realize they're talking about you?"

D0720197

MACK BOLAN

The Executioner

DON PENDLETON's EXECUTIONER
MACK BOLAN
Running Hot

A GOLD EAGLE BOOK FROM
W★RLDWIDE

TORONTO · NEW YORK · LONDON · PARIS
AMSTERDAM · STOCKHOLM · HAMBURG
ATHENS · MILAN · TOKYO · SYDNEY

First edition August 1985

ISBN 0-373-61080-7

Printed in Canada

Organized deceit occupies a central role in the conduct of Soviet foreign policy. The "active measures" department of the KGB, according to Western intelligence sources, is now running about one thousand deception operations every year, many of them dependent on agents of influence or "useful idiots" in the Western media and the political sphere.

—Robert Moss, *The KGB Lie Machine*

Terrorism is just a limited form of tyranny. The terrorist is a budding tyrant. Don't be taken in by his "freedom" rhetoric. He really means to dominate by force of arms— and always his intended victim is a free society.

—Mack Bolan

For the bravery and unstinting courage
of U.S. narcotics agent Enrique Camarena Salazar
and pilot Alfredo Zavala Avelar,
who were murdered in Guadalajara
by Mexican drug lords, February 1985.

1

The blood soaking the front of Mack Bolan's shirt was not his own. By the grace of whatever gods protect the brave, he had turned aside an instant before the car bomb exploded in the Paris street.

The newspaperman with Bolan was not so lucky. Facing the parked Peugeot 604 sedan when the wad of HMX plastique packed beneath the front seat was detonated, he was pummeled by the full force of the blast. From the searing fireball of erupting gasoline, a flying wedge of sheet steel scythed through the air and decapitated him as effectively as the blade of a guillotine.

Hurled backward, Bolan sat dazed on the sidewalk cradling a headless torso from whose severed neck a crimson stream jetted out over his chest in diminishing spurts.

He laid the warm corpse down and scrambled shakily to his feet. Bolan did not need a front-page headline in *Le Figaro* to tell him what had happened.

Yet another terrorist outrage.

Just one more senseless orgasm of violence and killing. World rule by the idiot fringe? Arab supremacy in the Middle East? Abolition of the state of Israel? Red power, black power, white power? Or was this just a simple protest against some political situation somewhere, anywhere? In France there were plenty of crackbrained fanatics to choose from. The country prided itself on being an asylum for political refugees.

Asylum was right, Bolan thought grimly. And some of the lunatics habored here were doing their best to turn the place into an abattoir.

Holdups, hijacks, the murder of hostages, booby-trapped automobiles, bombed airports and restaurants, assassinations in the streets with bystanders gunned down—the list was endless, someone had been slaughtered that way in the French capital in the past few months.

This particular hit was headed by Armenian extremists blowing the town apart in protest of atrocities committed by the Turks as long ago as 1916! Follow that as an example of logic, Bolan thought hopelessly.

But Bolan knew the present situation would be vastly preferable to the state of siege that would paralyze Paris and infect life in the whole of France if he did not successfully fulfill his current mission.

Fast.

He stared at the street. Brown smoke and brilliant flames rose from the devastated Peugeot, obscuring the shattered shop fronts. Shouts and screams filled the ear. It was the end of the lunch hour, casualties would be heavy.

Bolan and two men in tattered suits lifted a mangled motorcycle from the bloodied corpse of a woman across the road. The Executioner registered isolated details of the carnage: a bluish, steaming pile of guts and intestines lay strewn among the broken glass littering the macadam; a naked child wearing a single shoe sat crying beneath a broken balcony; leaves ripped from trees lining the street were still fluttering down through the smoke.

"Who the hell were they after this time?" a shocked café waiter asked a gendarme who was spreading his cape over something that resembled a bundle of bloodstained rags.

The cop surveyed the wrecked stores. "You tell me, friend." He shrugged. "There's a Turkish travel agency on this block, also a kosher restaurant, a left-wing bookshop, a Greek airline office. It could be any of them."

Mack Bolan turned away. The smoke was thinning. The blood on his shirt had caked in the heat: before the blast he had been enjoying a sunny spring day. The sun was still shining. Nearby, the bell of a burglar alarm set off by the explosion was shrilling relentlessly.

But it was not as loud as the alarm bells hammering in Bolan's mind.

The cop was entitled to his opinion, but Bolan was laying odds that the bomb had been intended for none of those places.

It had been specific, just the same. Hell yes, it had been specific.

Some driver had probably nudged the parked sedan just enough to actuate a trembler coil and fire the charge prematurely. A charge, Bolan figured, that should not have exploded until a key was twisted in the Peugeot's ignition.

The key in question, separated from a muscled thigh by a single layer of denim, lay in the right-hand pocket of his own jeans.

He had collected it early that morning when he rented the Peugeot at Charles de Gaulle Airport. If the terrorists' plan had not fouled up, Bolan would have been airborne again by now...in very small pieces.

2

"The briefing," Hal Brognola had announced some days before, "is simple." He placed an unlighted cigar in his mouth, taking some imaginary puffs before he continued.

Bolan chuckled inwardly as he took a sip of his beer. Hal had been trying to stop smoking for as long as Bolan could remember. These days it seemed as if the big Fed was winning.

They were sitting beneath a striped umbrella on a hotel terrace in Geneva. From a gray sky raindrops pockmarked the surface of the lake below.

"You could summarize the mission in three words, search and destroy," Brognola continued.

"Lay it on me," Bolan said. "Search where? Destroy what?"

Brognola did not reply directly. "I don't have to tell you, Striker, that terrorist activity globally is on the increase," he said. "Once, it was aimed at selected targets. Bad enough, but at least it made some kind of sense. Now it's indiscriminate and the hell with who gets hurt, know what I mean?"

Bolan knew. Sure he knew, as well as anyone could.

A lone Hercules, he had watched the Hydra grow. Ever since Vietnam, as the evil conspiracies of Animal Man increasingly threatened decent citizens, he had waged a relentless war against the enemy.

Bolan had undertaken thirty-odd bloodbath forays that had broken the Mafia's stranglehold on his own country, and innumerable battles against the forces of international terrorism. As a penetration specialist in Nam, and subsequently in his war against the Mafia, he had been known as The Executioner. Later, when the death toll had risen alarmingly and the pace had grown too hectic even for Bolan, he had undergone—with presidential approval—a staged death, plastic surgery, and a resurrection as Colonel John Phoenix, U.S. Army, retd. An unofficial employee of Uncle Sam.

As Phoenix, Bolan had masterminded a worldwide antiterrorist operation, covertly funded by the administration, from a secret location in Virginia's Blue Ridge Mountains. Brognola was the sole connection between Stony Man Farm, as it was called, and the White House.

But that was all over now.

For Bolan, the Stony Man operation was in the past.

Assassins from Russia's KGB, often the target on Stony Man missions, had blasted the farm in an attempt to eliminate Phoenix once and for all. They were unsuccessful, but a subsequent plot involving the murder of a respected European leader by a Bolan look-alike was not, and effectively put the Executioner beyond the pale.

Universally discredited, repudiated by his own country, Bolan had become an outlaw wanted by half the world's intelligence agencies.

That was the bad news. The good news was that now, as a loner answerable to nobody, he could choose his own targets, make his own plans, and strike when, where, how and as hard as he wanted.

It was an empty exercise to ask such a man if he knew about terrorists.

Between missions, Bolan had spent a lot of his time in the computer room at Stony Man checking repeatedly the global terrorist intel stored in the data banks of the powerful computer system run by Aaron Kurtzman.

After his disgrace, Bolan temporarily had access to an ultrahigh-tech associative memory system funded by an elderly Russian grand duchess and built in Paris by a scientist he had himself rescued from behind the iron curtain.

It was a while since Bolan had last heard from the duchess who, with some probing, had confessed that she was not in the best of health. And Bolan had promised himself to visit his ailing benefactress the moment he had some time.

The rebuilt Stony Man complex continued to be used as a base by Able Team and Phoenix Force, the antiterrorist squads Bolan had devised. Kurtzman, paralyzed from the waist down since the KGB assault, still presided over the computer consoles.

Despite Bolan's outlaw status, the Stony Man data banks remained at his disposal, thanks to the secret cooperation of the ever-loyal Kurtzman.

Brognola was something else.

Kurtzman offered the most sophisticated and comprehensive dossiers possible on the fanatics and extremists threatening the fabric of Western society. If Kurtzman represented intel, Brognola was policy. Through him, Bolan had an open line to the Sensitive Operations Group of the National Security Council and by extension to the White House.

If Brognola had violated the rules to secretly rendezvous with an outlaw four thousand miles from home, that had to mean action.

With a big *A*.

And however bitter Bolan felt about past betrayals, he would not ignore Uncle Sam's current request for help. He listened carefully to Brognola.

"France has been hardest hit in recent months," the big Fed was saying. "Diplomats gunned down, industrialists kidnapped, race riots fomenting, civilians zapped here, there and everywhere—France has had it all." He tapped a manila folder on the table between them. "And it's on the rise."

Bolan nodded. "And so?"

"So it's orchestrated," Brognola said.

"Orchestrated?"

"Each incident is part of a central master plan. French security intel agrees with Interpol and our own CIA and NSC findings. That means pretty conclusive evidence." Brognola crumpled the unsmoked cigar into an ashtray. "What do you know of Jules Treynet?" he asked abruptly.

Bolan's dark brows lifted. "Treynet? One of the world's richest men. Runs the aircraft corporation building France's AS-4 supersonic pursuit ship. Owns a shipping line, oil wells in the Sahara, mines in West Africa and numerous hotels in Europe."

"A man with a load of hate," said Brognola. "Nazi collaborator in World War Two. Recruited Fascist French to fight with the Nazis on the Russian front, things like that."

"Wasn't he jailed by a French war-crimes court?"

"Yeah. Ten years. But the guy has pull. He was out after eighteen months. Just in time to join up with extremists who tried to sabotage Algerian independence. He lost all his property there, never forgave the French for winning that war...and helping to win the one against Hitler."

Bolan frowned. "Agewise, he must be pushing it some."

"Sure. But he's passed the hate-mongering on to his son. It's Junior who organizes the bombers today."

"Are you saying that the Treynets are behind the terrorist outrage in France?"

"That's what I'm saying." Brognola held up an empty beer stein and signaled a waiter. "In ninety percent of the cases. The son, Jacques Edouard Treynet, operates this youth-club network. They use his initials, call themselves the JETs. With three million on relief in France, it's no sweat for the guy to recruit young hoodlums. And whatever political label they run, there's unlimited cash available to fund their attacks."

Bolan nodded again. "Okay, Hal, so what's the pitch?"

"It's a bad scene for the stability of Europe," Brognola said. "Therefore bad for the West as a whole. But there's nothing *we* can do, officially or unofficially. In any case, the

Man wants the Treynet operation exposed and destroyed. This is strictly unofficial. You never saw me. I was never here. But if that was to happen through you...well, let's just say a certain amount of heat might be turned off in other places. Do I make myself clear?''

"Right" was all Bolan said.

3

Search and destroy, right. Ever since Vietnam, those could have been the Executioner's watchwords, the credo by which he lived.

And others died.

Mack Bolan's personal crusade had always pitted him against the purveyors of evil and corruption. And the Executioner knew that the battle could only end when his own time came.

For Bolan's war admitted no armistice, no truce. You did not compromise with the Devil. He played by his own dark rules, and if you tried to beat him by using those rules, he changed them. For the Executioner, then, the fight was a continual performance.

With no intermission.

So search and destroy it was, yeah. Most times they went hand in hand. But for once, on this Paris deal, because there was not enough intel available on the quarry, the hunt would come first, the destruction later.

It wasn't the way he liked to play it, but if that was what they wanted...

"You hit Paris on a fact finder...as ordinary Joe Tourist with dollars to burn," Brognola had advised him.

Three days later Bolan found himself in France. Like any vacationer, he carried irrefutable ID papers, agency tickets and camera equipment. He also had an introduction to a Paris-based American newspaperman who was supposed to fill him in on the Treynet youth-club operation, though there was nothing in the letter to say this.

Yet less than four hours after his arrival, before the dollars had even begun to smoulder, the newspaperman was dead and Bolan's automobile booby-trapped and blown to hell.

So, it seemed, was his cover.

Okay, the hell with the pussyfoot routine. Bolan hated the defensive role anyway. If the enemy was wise to him and playing rough already, he would accept the challenge.

And strike before the bastards knew what hit them.

The JETs' official headquarters was a hutted summer camp not far from Lyons. Jacques Edouard Treynet owned a château nearby. His father contented himself with a Paris mansion in the snobbish sixteenth arrondissement. If the JETs' terrorist activities were planned for an operations center, Bolan figured it would be at the château rather than the camp.

He rented another car—a Renault 18 Turbo—and headed south that afternoon.

One hundred miles out of Paris he spotted the four guys in the Mercedes.

Bolan pedigreed them right off, their long hair and leather jackets out of place in the silver luxury sedan. ·

They made no attempt at concealment. He watched in the rearview mirror as they closed in on him along the sinuous ten-mile grade between the wooded Côte d'Or hills and the rolling vineyards of Burgundy.

The first attack came on the long, curving viaduct across the deep valley at Pont d'Ouche. Two hundred fifty feet above the valley's green fields and country lanes, Bolan was too busy negotiating the treacherous curves to pay any attention to the mirror. At seventy-five miles an hour, the legal limit on French highways, with a blustery crosswind buffeting the car, he needed to concentrate on the winding pavement. He was not aware the Mercedes had approached to within six inches of his rear bumper.

The big sedan surged forward and drew level with the rear tires of Bolan's Renault. Suddenly the driver of the Mercedes tugged the wheel sharply right and then left again.

It was expertly done. The heavy nose of the German car smashed once against the Renault's rear wheel, and then the aggressors had swerved wide and raced ahead to the far end of the viaduct.

The first thing Bolan knew of the assault was the unexpected lurch and stagger of his car as the impact slammed through its frame. The steering wheel spun out of his hands. The Renault skidded wildly and the front bumper clipped the balustrade of the viaduct and sent masonry crashing into the void.

A less experienced driver, panic-stricken, would have braked, spinning the sedan uncontrollably or sending it hurtling to eternity through the gap in the stonework. But the Executioner knew better than that. His foot had jerked instinctively toward the pedal but he willed it away, shifting down, then down again as the wheels grabbed the road and the rubber screeched protest into the sky.

Bolan fought the steering, wrenching the gyrating car back on course while it clipped the armco barrier separating the two lanes of the motorway, scraped the balustrade and finally zigzagged off the far end of the bridge with three of its four wheels still on the ground.

The young hoods were waiting unashamedly halfway up the hill on the far side of the valley. They were laughing.

As soon as the buckled Renault passed them, gathering speed again, the Mercedes pulled back onto the road and began to follow again.

Bolan pondered the situation. He wanted no shadows behind him when he headed for the hills.

Bolan grinned as an idea came to him. It pleased him because of its irony.

He would enlist the aid of the law. Yeah, but the law would not *know* it was on a bodyguard kick. He would fool the law into helping him...by breaking the law!

He started to push the needle around the clock face. The turbocharger growled as the Renault picked up speed from fifty...to sixty-five...to seventy. Behind him, the Mercedes swung wide to pass a line of trucks and took up position as before.

Bolan had not yet worked out how he would deal with the attackers if his plan worked. Traveling from Geneva with nothing but hand baggage on a normal Swissair flight, he had been obliged to arrive unarmed; passenger weapon checks were too tough to buck now that terrorist activity was so widespread.

He would fix the hardware problem once the mission entered the "destroy" phase.

Bolan had bought a "home defense" weapon from a gunsmith on the avenue de l'Opéra—an Arminius HW-7.GR revolver that was a replica of a Smith & Wesson Model 19 Combat Magnum.

The tiny pellets it fired would not stop a child at ten paces. But the muzzle blast could stun at very short range and the effect was frightening; the lead splinters produced extensive laceration and a lot of blood.

In any case—the Executioner mused, powering the Renault toward ninety—he should have no trouble putting the arm on four punks once he had them out of their vehicle.

Three more times the Mercedes attempted to force Bolan off the road. Twice its heavy-duty bumper smashed into the rear of the Renault, trying to nudge it into the bushes of the median strip. The third time, Bolan was sideswiped on an empty stretch of road.

The lighter French car spun twice with tires shrieking. It shot across the roadway, plowed through the soft earth of the median and careered backward into the northbound lane.

Bolan braked, wrestled the wheel, shifted, maneuvered the car out of the way of speeding traffic, finally jolting back through the bushes to his own lane. The Mercedes picked him up again half a mile down the road.

The turbocharger was screaming and the tachometer needle hit the red line when Bolan's plan paid off.

He saw the concealed patrol wagon, the cop with the radar gun as he flashed past a gap in the roadside shrubbery. As he expected, two men on motorcycles were waiting to flag him down around the next curve. They were CRS— *gendarmerie de la route*—very neat in white crash helmets, black leather jackets, black boots and white webbing belts. Clipped to the belts were holstered Browning automatics.

Bolan hurtled past, the powerful Mercedes drafting at his tail.

In his rearview mirror Bolan saw them yell into their radios and then, grim faced, kick their BMWs off the stands and give chase. They would be aiming now not only to bust him but to throw the book at him. If, when finally he allowed them to overtake him, he failed to produce any papers, then sure as hell they would take him to the nearest gendarmerie station for further questioning.

In effect, he would have an armed escort off the turnpike, and there would be nothing the punks could do about it.

It wasn't often that Bolan guessed wrong. This was one of the times.

He had underestimated the ruthlessness of the young hoods stalking him.

It was nearly five miles before the cops made it. As one BMW roared up alongside each car, the drivers gestured angrily toward the shoulder. Bolan pulled over and slowed. The turnpike here ran halfway up a swell of green hills beside the wine town of Macon. It was a clear sunny day; through a line of trees beyond the roofs and chimneys, the surface of the Saône gleamed blue.

The Executioner stopped and cut the engine. One of the cops dismounted ahead of the Renault and strode back, unbuttoning the flap of his breast pocket to drag out the note pad and ticket forms. The flap of the holster on his belt was already unfastened.

The Mercedes had halted fifty yards behind. Bolan glanced in the mirror and saw the cop walking toward it.

He was only halfway there when the big sedan leaped forward.

The cop didn't have a chance. He had time only to pivot, grab for his gun and open his mouth to yell before the gleaming grill smashed into him.

The impact tossed him spinning into the air, then he touched down again, the sedan thumping over his lifeless body.

The other patrolman froze beside the Renault.

That moment of hesitation cost him his life. He whirled, Browning in hand. Once, twice, three times the automatic spat flame. Crystal stars appeared on the Mercedes's windshield. But the big car was pushing forty and the cop had no place to go.

All Bolan could do was watch him die.

The sedan's right front fender punched into him, and threw him over the Renault, and onto the hard shoulder thirty feet away.

Bolan heard a sickening crunch as the officer's helmeted head hit concrete milepost. The Executioner knew the cop didn't stand a chance of survival.

The Mercedes hissed away, the youths still laughing.

Bolan cursed. He'd sure read that delinquent filth wrong.

These were no teenage dissuaders with orders to scare the shit out of a possible interloper. These were cold-blooded killers prepared to slaughter their way past the slightest obstacle.

Okay, Bolan thought grimly. He had been prepared to do a little dissuading himself, but now the name of the game had changed. Now the stakes were higher.

And there would be no replay.

With two policemen to be avenged, Bolan yearned for the blood of those punks.

Fifty yards ahead of the slain patrolman, a side road climbed a hill to a rest area where there was parking, numerous wooden tables for picnickers, and a small washroom in a grove. Bolan glanced back. In the distance, a knot of traffic was rapidly approaching. He decided to split before the bodies were discovered.

Ahead, the killers realized he was leaving the highway and began backing toward the rest area. The sun was sinking and most drivers were hurrying to arrive at their destinations before dark. Nobody was stopping for a picnic. When the Mercedes arrived at the restroom, only one car—the Renault—was parked there, and it was empty.

The youths piled out. From his hiding place, Bolan heard coarse guffaws, a heavy metallic crash, a liquid gurgle, and then the stunning bloomp of a gasoline explosion. A sheet of flame shot skyward.

They had overturned the Renault, opened the gas tank and ignited the leaking fuel.

That did it. All along, something had fazed the Executioner and now he knew what it was.

They were hopheads, spaced-out junkies with no power left to reason the results of their actions. He was dealing with mindless machines programmed to kill. Okay, he was not exactly inexperienced in killing himself.

The punks trooped into the restroom. One swung a length of bicycle chain, another a lead pipe, the two others unsheathed commando knives.

Twenty seconds later, they reemerged. "Creep musta lit and run," one of them said.

The bearded driver spit and snarled, "Naw, the lousy bum's wettin' his pants someplace in the bushes. Let's go flush the bastard out."

"Up here," Bolan called softly.

They fell back, startled, swearing, squinting upward. Bolan dropped from the branches of a tree growing against the washhouse, the Arminius alarm pistol in his left hand.

His right hand, rigid and plank hard, was poised to kill.

His feet struck one of the junkies on the shoulders, knocking him down. With the element of surprise in his favor, Bolan had sprung off the fallen killer and regained his balance before the others had time to close in.

He exploded into action. The odds were four to one, and that made it even, right.

To an onlooker unschooled in combat, the Executioner's windmilling arms and legs might have appeared undisciplined. In fact, each movement of every muscle was perfectly coordinated and planned with ice-cold precision. There were three men up and one down.

Bolan fired the pistol at the punk with the chain, not so much to disable him as to stop him in his tracks while the guys with the less dangerous weapons were dealt with. With his right foot he kicked the wrist of a hood brandishing a knife. With his right hand he chopped viciously down upon the skull of the man holding the lead pipe, slamming against the sphenoid area—one of the ten vulnerable karate points—six inches above the eyes. The ferocious impact jolted the punk's spine, tearing all the tomorrows off his calendar.

Bolan didn't stop. He whirled toward the man he had just kicked who had lost his knife and picked him up one-handedly, swinging him around as a shield. The bicycle chain flailed across his head and thwacked him into bloody unconsciousness.

Bolan threw the limp body at the chain guy and fired again at the hood rising from the ground who was preparing to disembowel him with his knife.

His snarl vanished behind a curtain of red. He fell screaming, clawing at his eyes.

The explosion of the small-bore pistol was still echoing among the trees when the junkie with the chain leaped in once more. The first shot had done no more than graze his cheek and lacerate one hand. Now that he realized the gun's limitations he was a hero again.

Bolan warded off a paralyzing blow to his forearm, numbing the wrist. Then, inside the killer's guard, he jammed the barrel of the pistol savagely against the hard-guy's mustache.

The killer jerked up his knee. Bolan twisted his groin away from the blow. A hand grappled with the hand holding the gun. Bolan immobilized it with a judo grip. "Okay, Junior," he panted, "this is it."

The Executioner had no qualms about what he was going to do next. The youth had callously murdered two men in front of him; he had probably killed before and would probably kill again if allowed to live. As he mouthed some obscenity and struggled to break away, the gun barrel drove into his mouth, smashing teeth.

Bolan squeezed the trigger.

The blast from the tiny .22 cartridge was not fierce enough to punch an exit wound, but the junkie fell with sufficient lead shot rattling around his skull to fill a pair of maracas.

It was almost dusk. Black smoke pulsing with crimson rose into the darkening sky from the burning Renault. Over the crackle of flames came the voices of motorists who had discovered the bodies of the cops.

The Mercedes was still running. Bolan slid behind the starred windshield and drove away.

4

It was almost dark when the Mercedes coasted to a halt outside a small village in the wooded hills northwest of Lyons. The Château des Azergues lay in an enormous tract of forest that had been planted as a game reserve by some medieval king of Burgundy. The main avenue, almost five miles long, could only be entered through the gate in a high wall at the edge of the village, across the road from a church and a garishly floodlit gas station.

A sign by the stack of new auto tires outside the gas station announced that La Colonie des Vacances Treynet—the summer camp that was the JETs' headquarters—lay ten miles to the west.

Bolan was still determined to try the château first. Since he always favored a frontal attack, he simply turned in the open gates and rolled sedately along the driveway.

If he had anticipated electric fences, guard dogs and armed thugs he was disappointed.

The driveway ran straight but the land undulated and it was never possible to see more than a few hundred yards between one crest and the next. The only sign of electrical work was a drum of cable standing at the roadside half a mile from the entrance. Beside it, evidently carrying new power lines to the château, was a tall concrete pylon bristling with insulators that flashed green in the sedan's headlights.

The car skidded to a stop and Bolan climbed out, taking a pair of insulated wire cutters from his hip pocket. He had

to take certain fail-safe precautions in case of a quick withdrawal. Ten minutes later he was back in the driver's seat.

The road passed a meadow laid out with brushwood
jumps for horse riders, then bridged a lake that snaked
through one of the hollows. But for the most part it ran
through a forest that pressed dark and close on either side.

Bolan drove for another ten minutes before he saw the big
house. Even then it was no more than a collection of lighted
windows that appeared successively larger each time he
topped a rise. When he was close he saw that the building
was immense: a huge symmetrical block of ocher sand-
stone with four turrets and a portico wide enough to shelter
the two Rolls-Royces behind its Corinthian pillars. A stable
block with a bell tower led off the driveway.

Bolan turned the Mercedes into the yard and left it facing the gates. He guessed the car was familiar to the château personnel.

He walked out of the yard and approached the château.
Stone steps rose from a formal garden to a terrace that ran
around one wing of the building.

Bolan sped silently up the steps and found that several sets
of French windows bordering the terrace were open. Diffused light from inside partly illuminated the facade.

Behind a closed picture window a brighter glow showed
between heavy draperies and he could hear the sound of
voices.

He eased open one of the French windows and stepped
into a dark room. On the far side, a thin rectangle of light
outlined a door that obviously led to an illuminated passage. He navigated around a sofa, several tables, an easy
chair, then opened the door. The corridor ran the whole
length of the wing. It was deserted.

If he'd read the signs correctly, the people were behind the
third door on his left. Glancing swiftly around, he moved
softly to the door and peered through the keyhole into the
lighted room.

He knew at once that the man standing in front of the vast carved chimneypiece must be one of his targets, the owner of the château.

Jacques Edouard Treynet wore a cream shantung suit, two-tone shoes, a Riviera tan and a thermonuclear smile. His bushy iron-gray hair was clipped as beautifully as a cypress hedge.

Lolling in white leather armchairs before him were four young men of the same type as the quartet in the Mercedes.

One of them was a fleshy hulk whose lopsided smile and vacant eyes suggested a stunted intelligence. Two were rat-faced punks with greasy hair. The fourth, a thin, wiry kid with unnaturally bright eyes and a discontented mouth, looked the most dangerous. Each of them was dressed in faded denims, basketball boots and a zippered Windbreaker.

"The most vital thing," Treynet was saying, "is that this snooper must on no account be allowed to leave the property. He's most likely the man Swanton fingered, but whoever he is, he must be eliminated. Is that clear, Bonzo?"

"Okay, okay," the thin boy said. "We'll take care of him, but good. Don't worry, Jacques."

"He already has the Merc, so he must have shaken the boys. If he was to learn anything about—if he even discovered the existence of the Eagle's Nest—"

"Forget it," Bonzo rasped. "Why don't you relax, J.E.? I told you we'd fix him."

Now the giant spoke. "Maybe there'd be...maybe there's somethin' you'd wanna find out first? Maybe you could use a little persuasion? You'll let me work him over some? Please?" His tone was wheedling.

"Patience, Moon. We'll turn the asshole over to you," Bonzo soothed. "For the last rites. Okay?"

He uttered a thin laugh and the two rat-faced kids giggled. It was not a pleasant sound. Bolan realized, staring at the fixed expressions and working lips, that these youths, too, were stoned out of their minds, ready for anything and damn the consequences.

"Whatever the details," Treynet said, "I insist that it must be...terminal."

Suddenly Bolan whirled, fingers reaching for the Arminius. A hand had touched his shoulder. A voice whispered in his ear, "You do realize they are talking about you?"

Bolan looked up to see a tall blonde in a flowered silk dress standing behind him. He hesitated for a heartbeat, not sure what to make of the newcomer.

"You walked into a trap," the woman said in a low voice. "There are well-hidden sensors all along the driveway. The Mercedes packs a UHF transmitter that signals its arrival, and up here the place is lousy with infrared video cameras. They know all about you."

The Executioner glanced at the alarm pistol and shook his head. Without the element of surprise and, with his every move tracked, the odds didn't look so favorable this time.

"You must leave at once before Bonzo and the others quit the library and Treynet returns to his screens," she urged.

"Where—and what—is the Eagle's Nest?"

"Something we don't talk about. Come. Quickly." She led the way to the far end of the corridor. Bolan followed her through a kitchen garden to an orchard that stretched as far as the stable. As they traversed a shaft of light slanting through one of the windows, he watched her move, a slender, curvaceous woman who glided so gracefully within the silk sheath that he knew she must be naked beneath it.

"I'm grateful," he said. "So who *are* you?"

She made no reply, but he sensed that she was smiling in the dark. At length she said, "There's a Lambretta scooter against the wall at the entrance to the stable yard. Take it and leave quickly. The other bikes are very powerful."

"Other bikes? Why would I need—"

The blonde cut him off. "Moon is the worst kind of sadist. But they are all very cruel. And they would probably

catch you, even if you got out of here alive. They have contacts in every village around here.

"If I leave in the Merc—"

"I don't think so. But whatever you do, act fast." She
touched his arm, then slipped away between the forest trees
growing at the edge of the orchard.

"Hey!" Bolan called. "Why would I need a scooter?"

But there was no answer. He heard a rustle of leaves and
then silence. Back at the château, a door slammed.

Bolan moved cautiously to the stable yard, his mind see-
thing with unanswered questions. How had the terrorists
gotten on to him so soon after his arrival in Paris? How had
they known he was coming, and perhaps even why he was
coming? How did the Mercedes come to terrorize him up on
the highway? Who was Swanton? Most importantly, who
was this mysterious blonde, why had she helped him, and
what the hell did she mean, going on about the Mercedes
and some scooter?

The last question was answered almost at once.

Beneath the bell tower, a small overhead lamp had been
illuminated. In the diffused light, Bolan saw that the air had
been let out of the sedan's tires: all four wheels were flat.

He cursed under his breath, moving silently into the
shadows at one side of the gateway. The little scooter was
there, all right. Beyond it, glinting through the darkness,
were four powerful motorcycles.

So these were the other bikes the woman had been talking about. Treading lightly on the cobbles, he looked them
over. A Harley-Davidson, a 4-cylinder Gold Wing Honda
and two 1100cc Yamaha machines.

Bolan almost laughed out loud as he envisioned himself
on the scooter. The hell with it. He would take the Honda.
It was the fastest, 140 plus.

Seconds later, he realized why the blonde's suggestion had
been a good one. The four bikes were chained to a metal
hitching post, the scooter wasn't. And even if he had time,
he had nothing with which to pick the locks.

He crept toward the scooter…and froze.

Someone was walking into the yard.

Bolan saw the glow of a cigarette, and then, as the figure passed into the pool of lamplight, the silhouette of a man carrying a heavy nightstick. He wasn't one of the four junkies. This was a husky, barrel-chested guy in his forties. Clearly he had been sent to guard the bikes but thanks to the blonde, Bolan had beaten him to it. Just.

There was no time to check the guy out. Bolan moved up behind him with the alarm pistol held at arm's length. It was either a soft football or the tiny metallic click of the cocking hammer as the cylinder rotated, but something in the last hundredth of a second alerted the guard and he began to turn.

Bolan shot him in the nape of the neck, the muzzle of the gun an inch from the gap between his collar and his hair.

At that range with no spread, the pistol would stun but not kill. Bloodied, the guy dropped to the ground.

Bolan frisked him. Surprisingly, apart from the weighted baton, he was unarmed. Too bad, though. The Executioner could have used a real gun if those punks were coming after him.

He shrugged. What the hell. For once he'd have to operate without weapons. Certain arrangements he had made on the way in would have to help him out now. He kicked the Lambretta to life and roared out of the yard and down the avenue.

He did not ride as far as the gates. Just before reaching the new electricity pylon, he steered the scooter off the dirt road and into a clearing screened by dense undergrowth. He had to be hidden before the pursuers appeared over the previous rise.

He had crawled to the grassy shoulder when the thunder of exhausts split the night. A moment later they materialized—dim black shapes behind the glare of headlamps, sinister against the somber forest background.

The four were bunched, riding like the wind. They must have been hitting eighty or ninety when they drew abreast of Bolan, engines screaming.

A split second later, Bonzo, slightly in the lead on the howling Honda, ran full tilt into the almost invisible electric cable that Bolan had strung across the driveway on his approach to the château.

The junkie hellhound had just turned his head to yell some obscenity at his buddies when the wire, vibrating neck-high between the tree trunks on either side of the road, caught him squarely across his bared throat.

It sliced through his neck and spinal column, sending his lifeless head spinning high into the air while the Honda roared crazily on with the decapitated body fountaining blood from its severed neck.

One was for the newspaperman who had died in Paris.

A heartbeat later, the vast leather-clad Moon, riding slightly higher on the Harley-Davidson, hit the wire. Caught across his gorilla shoulders, the retarded hophead was flung from the saddle as the machine reared up screeching from the trail.

A foot touched the ground...and a searing blue flash lit the night as the high-voltage current jolted through the rider. For a terrible instant his entire form—open mouth, curling hair, wispy beard, splayed arms and legs—was limned in crackling fire. Then the cable snapped, he crashed to the ground, the bike fell on the electrocuted corpse and fuel from the split tank exploded with a dull roar.

Simultaneously the first of the Yamahas reached the second of the three wires Bolan had fixed at ten-yard intervals. The taut cable struck the crouched rider on top of his bent head, slicing deep into his skull, down through the ears to break the neck instantly. His body somersaulted into the bushes lining the driveway as the bike erupted into a ball of fire and another vivid flash fused the second wire.

A few yards behind the others, Ratface No. 2 had time to jerk upright, even brake a little before he ran into the third wire. Even so, he was still traveling at more than seventy miles an hour.

There was a sound that resembled the twanging of a monstrous bow. The second Yamaha, freed of its load, careered off to one side and into a tree. The rider, catapulted with maniac force by the electrified cable, flew through the night to thump down near the Executioner's feet. A scarlet geyser spurted rhythmically from his neck.

Bolan pushed himself upright. The cold fury that had consumed him since the slaughter of the highway patrolmen was now spent. It might not be such a bad thing, educating the slimeballs in the perils of crime.

A crash course, right.

Bolan surveyed the carnage. Ratface No. 1 was draped across a rhododendron bush ten yards from the driveway.

On the roadway, garishly lit by the flames billowing from the ruins of the Harley-Davidson, Moon's body, charred and unrecognizable, was still being licked by tongues of flame.

Bonzo's machine and its decapitated rider had plowed on for nearly a hundred yards. The motorcycle was lying, twisted and battered, beside the headless corpse. The engine was still turning, the rear wheel spinning uselessly. He leaned down and cut the fuel supply, hearing in the sudden quiet nothing but the menacing crackle of flames.

Beyond the wrecks of the two Yamahas, Ratface No. 2 lay in the long grass by the roadside.

Evidently he had gotten wise to the danger and had leaned sideways at the last moment in a futile effort to escape the invisible death strung across the road; the wire had slashed diagonally upward from his upper arm to the top of his neck.

There was still a flicker of life in the youth's dull eyes.

He left the punk to die, donned rubber gloves and began to dismantle the sophisticated hookup he had contrived at the pylon. A few minutes later he removed the remnants of the murderous cables from the trees and concealed them in the undergrowth.

Let Treynet and his hirelings figure out what bloody vengeance had destroyed their team.

By the time he had finished, the flames had died down and a deep silence brooded over the windless dark of the forest. So far there had been no sign of further pursuit from the château.

The Executioner mounted the Lambretta and rode away.

The next step was to check out the Eagle's Nest, whatever that was. But before he moved again, Bolan was going to be equipped with proper weapons and the right kind of rig.

This was supposed to have been no more than a soft-probe. Well, he had enough facts now to justify something a mite more aggressive.

Soon Treynet and his terrorists would be faced with a one-man wave of destruction.

5

The JETs' summer camp lay in four hundred acres of woodland between Roanne and Vichy, in central France. Bolan figured the site was well chosen: Vichy had been the headquarters of Pétain's pro-Nazi French during World War II. Maybe the air was still contaminated.

The site had been chosen well for another reaosn.

The woods crowned a swell of high ground separating two valleys, and the property could be overlooked only from the hilltops beyond those valleys—too far away for any casual rubbernecks to see what went on inside, even if they had binoculars.

Mack Bolan was no casual rubberneck.

He did have binoculars—along with the camera, zoom lens and travel guides that were part of his tourist cover—but no way could they be related to the kind of field glasses carried by the average tourist.

They were twinned Trilux IR/4 telescopic nightsights designed for rifle marksmen, framed in a converted Zeiss housing of the pattern once used by German U-boat commanders. The rig had been assembled—with certain high-tech modifications—by Andrzej Konzaki, the Stony Man armorer who had been seconded from the Special Weapons Development branch of the CIA. Konzaki, one of the world's most inventive weaponsmiths, had been killed in the terrorist attack on the farm.

It seemed fitting that one of his specialties should be used to expose more slime of the kind responsible for his death.

Yeah, Bolan thought coldly, the missile may be a long-time flyer, but eventually there will be a hit. And when there is, no stone will be big enough for the vermin to crawl under.

Invisible himself, he would use those infrared binoculars after dark from a vantage point on one of those hills. But first he was going to recon the Treynet camp in daylight and at close quarters.

The property was surrounded by a ten-foot chain link fence, and the undergrowth and trees behind it grew so densely that nowhere was it possible to see into the interior. The way in—there was only one—was more like the entrance to a military installation than a vacation camp. Stark white lines delineated the forecourt parking lot, in the middle of which was a graveled semicircle with a flagstaff at the center. A French tricolor with the JETs' monogram logo hung from the mast.

Beyond the forecourt, tall barred gates stood open behind a striped barrier pole. Two uniformed guards with holstered revolvers stood by the barrier; a third carrying a shotgun was visible through the window of a gatehouse.

Bolan parked his third rental car—another Peugeot—and strolled to the gates. Inside, a narrow road skirted a wooden building that looked like an administration block and then twisted behind several groups of huts among the trees.

The two guards watched Bolan approach the barrier. They were heavy, bull-necked men about forty years old. With their cropped hair and expressionless faces, they reminded him more of Family enforcers in Chicago or Detroit than gatekeepers in provincial France.

"What do you want?" the taller one demanded gruffly when Bolan was half a dozen yards away.

Bolan was fluent enough, but he could not pass for a Frenchman. He said, "I represent an American electronics company in Lyons. I have to travel a lot in summer. I was wondering if my son—"

"No more vacancies this year," the shorter man interrupted.

"That so? Well, maybe next Christmas or Easter?"

"The place is all booked up through August of next year," the shorter guy said.

"That's too bad." Bolan was now a few feet from the guards. "Just the same, I guess I'll go have a word with the front office. I like to plan ahead, and I imagine they have brochures and that kind of thing?" He made as if to step over the barrier.

The taller man blocked his way. "Nobody gets in here," he said curtly, eyeballing the Executioner, "without an okay signed by the director."

"But I wanted to ask...surely..."

"The office is open visiting days. That's Monday and Thursday. Today's Wednesday."

"But I've come all the way from Lyons—"

"We have a bureau in Lyons," the short hood said. "In Paris, too. That's where you ask questions. The bosses don't like folks nosing around here whenever they want. We got young kids in here. Like we're responsible. We can't have just anybody—"

"What kind of a story are you handing me?" Bolan exploded, allowing himself a pretense of anger.

"I figure it's time you was leavin'," the tall man said.

"Hell, I only wanted to ask—"

"Anyways, this camp is for poor kids got no other place to go. It's like subsidized: you can't buy your way in here." The guard stared at Bolan's clothes. At six-two and 200-odd pounds, even in a faded denim jacket and jeans, no way could the big guy look underprivileged.

"Look, I demand to see the director," Bolan blustered.

"You ain't in no position to demand anythin'," the shorter man said. "This is private property. We let in who we like, we keep out who we like. On your way now, mister. Get goin'."

For an instant Bolan's muscles tensed. It was tough, taking this kind of talk from scum. His fingers clenched, and then gradually relaxed. It wasn't part of his plan to wise up the hired help that he meant trouble.

Not yet.

The guard's hand had dropped to the holster clipped to his belt. "Are you goin' to get the hell out, or do I have to call the monitors to run you off the site?" he threatened. The guy with the shotgun stepped out of the hut, cradling the weapon.

"I don't understand why you—"

"Beat it."

The shotgun advanced toward the barrier. Bolan turned on his heel and strode back to the Peugeot.

As he maneuvered the car out of the parking space he took a final look past the gates. Beyond the huts he could see the tops of tents among the trees, but most of the accommodation visible was trailers strung out on each side of the road.

Any compromising stuff, he reckoned, would be in those. They could be hauled away quickly, contents undisturbed, in case of emergency.

The few campers he had seen in the distance while he argued with the gate men had all been adolescents. There would be no place here for the eight- to twelve-year-olds that French parents customarily packed off to vacation camp between school semesters. That figured with what Brognola had told him. But...restricted to poor kids? Kids from broken homes, more likely. Delinquents, probationers, orphans, parole-board cases. They would be the natural material for Treynet's kind of brainwashing.

As for the activities within the camp, apart from the fact that strangers were not welcome, he had learned only one thing: in the distance he had heard gunfire.

And the shots were from heavy-caliber handguns interspersed with volleys that could have come only from automatic-assault weapons—machine pistols or submachine guns.

Clearly Brognola had been handing him no fairy tale.

Maybe tonight, installed on that hilltop, he would find out more. There must be open spaces among those trees. Once he had located them, Konzaki's night-vision rig should help him discover what was going on in the camp.

He was about to turn onto the highway when the barrier pole rose and a group of about twenty bikers rode out of the camp. Behind the visored crash helmets, their features were invisible, but the bodies, sporting ski jackets, Windbreakers and black leather jackets studded with metal, looked husky. Most of the machines were powerful 4-cylinder models, from 750cc upward.

They swirled arrogantly past Bolan, so close that the wheels kicked up gravel to hammer the Peugeot's body panels on either side. Before he could react they roared off toward the nearest village, exhausts bellowing through clouds of dust.

Soon after dark, Bolan parked the car and started the long climb to a rock outcrop he had figured to be the best place to overlook the Treynet property. He was wearing his combat blacksuit and a silenced Beretta 93-R harnessed near the sheathed commando knife beneath his left arm. There were concussion grenades clipped to the webbing just below his shoulder, and "Big Thunder," the stainless-steel .44 AutoMag that was Bolan's favorite headblaster, was holstered low on his right hip.

Smuggling the weapons into France had been no sweat. Brognola had sent them in a diplomatic pouch, and an embassy messenger had left it unopened for Bolan to pick up at the American Express office behind the Paris opera. It was still less than three days since the explosion had wrecked his car in the street.

The hillside was steep, strewn with loose stones beneath clumps of coarse grass, heather and furze. It was a dark night, not cold, with a light breeze carrying the scent of thyme and broom.

Once on the outcrop, Bolan slid Konzaki's binoculars from their case. He focused on the wooded dome below.

And of course there were open spaces. The trees had been concentrated on the perimeter to block prying eyes.

Bolan swung the glasses from left to right, scanning the terrain. The moonscape wanly illuminated by the red Triphium light source was alive with activity.

Kids, girls as well as boys, jogged around a small cinder track, yelled at by a monitor if they didn't make it up to speed. Some of the youths were muscled, some looked spindly and undernourished, and most were between these extremes. Their ages, Bolan guessed, ranged from thirteen to seventeen, though most of the girls looked fairly mature.

The floodlit shooting range was no more than 120 or 130 yards long. Here older kids crouched, knelt, stood or in some cases took running shots at the targets. But instead of the usual concentric circles, these were cutout silhouettes of automobiles, bikes and human figures, moving at varying speeds across the banked sand in front of them. Bolan's hearing had not been at fault earlier in the day; the weapons used were handguns and machine pistols.

In another clearing, thirty or forty boys practiced unarmed combat. Nearby, separate groups wielded riot sticks, balks of wood and slingshots in what looked like a pitched battle against uniformed men with visors and shields. Trainers stood on the sidelines shouting instructions through bullhorns.

Through the twin Trilux rig with its object-glass, prism-lens and eyepiece assemblies unobstructed by cross hairs or vertical-aiming pointers, Bolan saw that there were no punches pulled. These kids were playing rough.

At the far end of the estate, more than half a mile from the gates, Bolan saw a twisting switchback of interlaced dirt roads on which jalopies and trail bikes bounced and swung in a crazy mixture of motocross and a dodgem rally. Bolan could hear the rasp of overgunned engines, the clang and crunch of buckled metal from the far side of the valley.

The most surprising program was on the other side of the dome. Beyond some kind of unlit obstacle course, an old house stood in a glade between eucalyptus and plane trees. It was a big rambling place with three stories and an attic floor. At first Bolan did not make the connection.

The crumbling facade appeared to be pulsing with movement.

He figured there must be some anomaly with the nightsight, a trick of the infrared, maybe. Then he saw that his first impression had been correct.

There *was* movement all over the facade. Antlike in their numbers and complexity, groups of the JETs were swarming up eaves troughs, balanced on the guttering, jimmying windows, lowering ropes from the roof, edging along a three-inch ledge that traversed the building at the third-floor level.

There were cars, vans and trucks parked along the road that ran past the house. As he watched, three youths and a girl burst from the porch and backed down the steps, firing submachine guns as they retreated. A beat-up sedan moved into sight, braked while the quartet piled in, and then accelerated fiercely away, zigzagging between the parked vehicles. It was followed at once by a vehicle with a flashing blue light on its roof. Bolan tracked them through the trees until they reached the motocross complex.

He lowered the glasses and drew a deep breath. There could be no doubt about it now. What he had seen clinched it.

He had found a sophisticated course in urban-guerrilla techniques. Those kids were being taught to handle antipersonnel weapons, to fight dirty and deadly. They were being exercised in the black arts of burglary and break-ins.

After the simulated holdups and getaways, he knew that what was going on down there were dress rehearsals for hijackings, armed robberies and other acts of terror. He had discovered a training ground for terrorists.

Vacation camp, hell! Bolan thought. What those bastards are running is a school for slaughter....

Later, from a different vantage point, he looked down on the extracurricular activities of the inmates. He heard the blare and thump of hard rock from a big marquee near the house. Monitors circulated handing out sachets of white powder, syringes, smokes. The kids were snorting and shooting. Pretty soon, he knew, they'd be screwing, too— encouraged by the monitors.

The music grew wilder, louder. The boys and girls began pairing off and wandering back to the tents and trailers. Sometimes a girl would have more than one boy with her. Once or twice giggling groups began to strip among the trees.

It was two o'clock before the music stopped. Soon afterward, Bolan heard a girl scream. Then the lights went out and there was silence in the valley.

His face was grim as he packed the nightsights into the case and threaded his way back down the scrub-covered slope.

He got into the Peugeot and switched on the engine. For a long time he sat behind the wheel, pondering the operation he had uncovered, examining the alternatives that were open to him as the next move. Then he eased the short T-shaped lever into Drive and steered out of the disused gravel pit where he had parked.

He was turning onto the highway when he became aware of movement behind him. Before he could react, he felt cold steel jammed against the back of his neck. "All right, smart ass," a hoarse voice growled. "You were told we don't like snoopers here. But if it's so goddamn important that you see inside the camp, well I guess the best thing is we take you there. Now you drive back to the main gates, slow and easy."

The gun barrel moved abruptly, jolting Bolan's head forward. "But you step one inch out of line," the voice warned, "and I'll blow your fucking head off."

6

The Executioner was not in the normal way an angry man; the fury powering his campaign against the evil that threatened the security of the world was cold and calculated. He rarely lost that cool and he was much too good a soldier to allow his tactics or strategy to be affected by emotional factors.

Only twice in his life had a hot-tempered thirst for vengeance and retribution menaced this icy determination. The first time was when he was called from Vietnam on compassionate grounds to find his parents and sister dead because of a Mafia intrigue. It unleashed his personal, successful—but illegal—crusade against the barons of organized crime.

The second terminated his Stony Man career after April Rose, the love of Bolan's life, paid the supreme price during the attack on the farm to save him from an assassin's bullet. The killer had died. And later Bolan had liquidated the Washington mole responsible for the siege in the Oval Office before the eyes of the President.

He could not ride that one out. No administration could look the other way on that one. And Bolan already had enemies and would-be rivals in the intelligence community. That was why he was now an outlaw.

But outlaws do not necessarily lose their beliefs, and Mack Bolan was a believer. He believed in decency and democracy and truth and justice.

Maybe this was why, face-to-face with the Treynets' plans to corrupt a whole generation, Bolan felt within him for the third time the rise of that choking anger that threatens to stifle all rational thought.

Driving back to the main gates of the vacation camp, he tried to stifle his rage.

Already it had been responsible for an uncharacteristic lapse on his part: there had been two guys crouched behind the front seats of the Peugeot. He blamed the rising tide of his wrath for the fact that he had been caught unawares because he had failed to check the car.

Big Thunder and the Beretta had been unleathered by the second man as soon as they were on the highway. Afterward he leaned over and unclipped the grenades, withdrew the knife from its sheath.

"Hey, I was only—" Bolan began.

"Shut up and drive," the gunman snapped.

Bolan knew those voices. He had been taken by the two guards who had blocked him that morning.

This time the gates were open. The bar was raised. They stopped beside the administration block. "Up the steps and through the door," the man with the gun said. "Hands clasped on top of the head, and no tricks."

Each of the hoods was armed with a Walther PPK, Bolan saw as he climbed out from behind the wheel. They moved warily, leaving him no chance to dive beneath the Peugeot or duck behind a door. The one toting Bolan's own artillery shouldered open the door and jerked his head. "Inside and first right," he ordered.

The wind had freshened. Before he entered the building, Bolan saw a flicker of lightning smear the western sky. A moment later thunder rumbled in the distance.

The room Bolan was shoved into was some kind of an office. He blinked in the glare of fluorescent lighting. He saw gray steel filing cabinets, a glassed-in notice board, a PBX telephone switchboard. Behind the bare top of a broad metal desk two men sat facing the door.

Jacques Edouard Treynet and a heavy, new to Bolan.

The second guy was enormous, taller than Bolan, carrying maybe forty pounds more weight, all of it muscle. His head was shaved, and he had small eyes set in a face like a slab of granite.

The taller guard dropped Bolan's weapons and binoculars on the desk. He unbuckled the harness and laid that on top of them.

Treynet smiled. The white teeth flashed. "I think an explanation would be in order, Bolan," he said softly.

Bolan stared. How the hell had the guy found out his name? Even if they had tailed him back to the village inn where he was staying and searched his room, they would have found nothing that didn't stack up with his cover identity. But clearly, armed and dressed in a combat suit, he wasn't going to get away with any pretense. Playing for time he said, "I don't think we've met."

"Not officially," the Frenchman agreed, "although you have been in my house, I believe."

Bolan said nothing.

Treynet was wearing a midnight-blue, mohair two-piece suit with a Pucci scarf tucked into the open neck of a white silk shirt. "The police will deal with that in due course," he said, flicking a speck of dust from his lapel. "But first, certain questions require answers."

"Yours or mine?" Bolan countered.

Treynet ignored the interruption. "We know all about you, you see. We know who you are and what you are." The smile this time was almost a sneer. "Citizen Mack Bolan, alias Sergeant Mercy, alias Colonel John Phoenix, alias the Executioner. An assassin, a mercenary, a gun for hire, a self-appointed do-gooder. We know also that you are now an outlaw, on the kill list of half the world's intelligence agencies. A man, as they say, with a price on his head. What we don't know is why you are here."

Treynet paused and regarded Bolan levelly. "You are a man on the run," he said. "No organization that could make trouble for me is going to employ you. So why do you, as a loner, choose to meddle in my affairs? In fact, that is really the only question that remains to be answered. Why?''

Bolan hesitated. He resisted the temptation to reveal how much he knew about Treynet and how much he detested what he knew. Outside the building the thunder grumbled again, nearer this time. At length Bolan said, "You mentioned the police?''

"Certainly I did. Once you have told us what we want to know—and ultimately, you *will* tell us—once we have that information, we shall hand you over and prefer charges.''

"No kidding?'' Bolan said. "On what charges?''

"Murder, for a start,'' said Treynet. "You butchered four young men who were guests in my house. Four innocent lads out for a spin on a spring evening.''

Bolan saw no point in playing dumb. Not at this stage. "We may have different interpretations of the term 'innocent,''' he said. "In any case, there is nothing to connect me with those...accidents.''

"Your fingerprints are all over the cable, the drum, the electricity pylon, even the wrecked machines.''

Bolan shook his head. "Who are you trying to kid, Treynet? I'm making no admissions, but whoever rigged that trap was wearing rubber gloves. So no prints.''

"You were not wearing gloves when you broke into the château and eavesdropped on my private conversations. And apart from that burglary there is the theft of a Lambretta scooter, an unprovoked assault with a firearm on a member of my staff, the matter of trespass.''

Bolan was favored with another smile. "A case takes a long time to come to trial in this part of the country. Also, I have some...shall we say...influence with the local police captain. I would think there is enough here to keep you in jail at least until the trial. By which time my plans will be complete and you will no longer be a nuisance, even if they acquit you.''

The giant sitting next to Treynet spoke for the first time. "Leave the bastard to me," he growled. He spoke French with a strong German accent. "I'll beat the answer out of him in ten minutes. After that I'll break his back and we'll fix a hit-and-run scenario someplace on the Vichy turnpike."

Bolan looked the man over again. Beneath a white T-shirt printed with the JETs' logo, his body was as solid as a kung fu master's.

Nice guy. Good company.

"I'll explain it once more, Lange," Treynet said. He paused. There was a loud crash of thunder and the lights dimmed momentarily. "It's good for our image," Treynet resumed. "We turn in a man wanted by half the law enforcement agencies in the world. We have been the victims of unprovoked aggression by a proven killer. Very properly, instead of taking the law into our own hands, as we might justifiably do, we call in the duly appointed guardians of the peace. Indirectly this man's crimes whitewash us. It strengthens the picture of the JETs as a law-abiding organization."

Bolan had been sizing up possible exits from the room. Between him and the entrance door, the two guards were still standing with drawn guns. There was another door, leading to an inner office, but it was directly behind Lange. No escape there! The steel skirt of the desk came right down to the floor. Two windows, tongued and grooved, opened inward in the French style. Beyond them, pairs of slatted wooden shutters were secured with metal hooks and eyes. Wood rattled and glass vibrated as the thunder roared for the third time. Abruptly rain began to fall, drumming on the asphalt roof.

Treynet looked at the gold Rolex on his wrist. "We have other things to do," he said. And to Lange, "I shall call the police in fifteen minutes. Take Bolan into the other room. I shall expect to have the answer—why the interfering fool is getting in my way—before I dial the number."

Lange pushed himself to his feet, eyeing the Executioner. He flexed his fingers. Muscles rippled beneath the T-shirt. "It will be a pleasure," he said.

Bolan was aware of the guards behind him tensing in expectation of some resistance on his part.

The building shook to an appallingly loud thunderclap and all the lights went out.

In the blackness Bolan dived. He scooped harness, binoculars and the two guns from the desk and dropped to the floor. Flame stabbed the dark as the two PPKs hosed lead in his direction.

"Not this way, you cretins!" Treynet yelled, plummeting with Lange on the far side of the desk. Glass from the notice board shattered and fell as the slugs sprayed the wall.

Bolan reached up for the window catch and heaved with all his strength, breaking the catch and yanking the windows toward him. The Walthers spat fire again, but he was already on his feet beside the desk. He took three swift steps and leaped, right foot kicking out horizontally karate-style. But instead of an opponent's jaw, the sole of his combat boot struck the latch fastening the shutters with stunning force.

The hook tore away from the eye, and Bolan hurtled through in a shower of splintered wood and broken glass.

He was on his feet and running through the rain before his captors reached the smashed window.

Another peal of thunder. The lights came on again, silhouetting the two guards in the frame.

Bolan had Big Thunder in his right hand, the safety off. He blasted two flesh-shredding rounds and dodged behind the Peugeot. One of the guards vanished backward, half his head blown away by the impact of the .44 blockbuster.

Everything now depended on the car. Had the guards been professional enough to lift the keys from the ignition?

Bolan jerked open the door on the side away from the building. They hadn't.

He threw in his gear, thrust himself behind the wheel, and loosed off two more shots at the second guard, who had dropped to the flower bed beneath the window. Glass in the Peugeot's side window imploded as the man fired. But the death spray from the AutoMag punctured his chest and slammed him against the side of the building.

Bolan twisted the key. The still-warm engine caught at once and he gunned the car around in a U-turn.

Treynet appeared at the window, gripping a pistol in both hands. Lange burst through the entrance door and leaped down the steps. But Bolan was long gone, thundering toward the gates. Grabbing vainly for a door handle, the German giant fell on his face behind the car. Treynet's shots thunked into the trunk, shattered the rear window, then dropped away.

Nearing the gates, Bolan saw two more guards run from the hut and start hauling the heavy iron portals shut. The barrier pole was already barring the roadway.

Bolan put his foot down.

The Peugeot leaped forward.

The guards, seeing that they weren't going to make it with the gates, dropped to crouching positions, machine pistols at the ready.

Bolan steered with one hand, knocking glass from the splintered window with the barrel of the AutoMag. Aiming the car at the nearest man, he emptied the remaining rounds in the magazine at the other. One of the 240-grain slugs zapped the gateman between the eyes, knocking him flat on his back three yards away, the top of his head pried open like a can of spaghetti.

The second guard opened fire on full auto. Bolan heard the snarl of the machine pistol over the howl of the Peugeot's engine. The windshield starred once more. And again. Lead whammed into the hood, the lamps, screeched off a wheel. Then the bumper punched into the guy hip-high, smashing the machine pistol up into his face, tossing him aside like a lightweight mannequin.

Two seconds later there was a jarring shock as the buckled front of the car hit the outside end of the barrier pole.

The pole snapped like a matchstick and spun high into the air. The Peugeot lurched, righted itself, shed glass and chrome over the wet pavement. And then Bolan was through.

As he hit the highway, a group of bikers roared into sight and wheeled across the gravel lot toward the gates. They were laughing, singing, riding on rear wheels with the fronts high in the air, cavorting like riders possessed.

Or hopheads on a high.

Bolan left them to it. He turned the battered Peugeot the other way, collected his kit from the village inn, and drove back to Paris. There was a hell of a lot to think over before he could make the next move.

7

The last passenger to leave the Lufthansa flight from Frankfurt that Thursday was Herr Doktor Dieter Schmitt-Heinkel. Evidently he was a regular client, for the cabin crew all smiled and wished him a pleasant stay in Paris as he stepped through the hatch onto the flexible gangway that linked the plane with the terminal, and even the Air France girl behind the arrivals desk nodded a welcome.

Charles de Gaulle Airport, at Roissy, a dozen miles north of Paris, is thought by some to be the crowning glory of contemporary industrial architecture. Others complain that its tubular Plexiglas escalators and transparent scaffolding make it look like an unfinished experiment in a chemical laboratory. Whichever, the design is functional. It works. One of the high-speed walkways had carried Schmitt-Heinkel to the central core of the building, his single holdall safely past the security scanners, his German passport stamped and returned, within seven minutes of the plane's touchdown.

He walked briskly through the crowds thronging the circular passageway, past banks, bars, gift shops and airline desks, until he found a row of telephones that were unoccupied.

He took the instrument beneath the right-hand acoustic dome, fed in four five-franc pieces, and dialed. When the receiver at the other end was lifted, the first coin was accepted, leaving three visible in a transparent panel beneath the insert slots.

"Schmitt-Heinkel. Let me talk to Treynet," the German said.

He waited for the connection to be made, tapping one foot impatiently—a bulky man with curly white hair and heavy jowls.

The Herr Doktor was chairman of a small but increasingly vociferous neo-Fascist political party in Bavaria, and was slated for a seat in the local *bundestag* after the coming cantonal elections.

He was also, with Jacques Edouard Treynet, joint director of the Franco-Teuton Bund, an extreme right-wing "friendship" organization with headquarters in Paris.

"Ici Treynet. Je vous écoute." The Frenchman's voice was deep and pleasantly modulated.

"Hello? J.E.? Dieter. I am in Paris. No problems. The onward flight is in two hours time. I should be at the Eagle's Nest for dinner."

He listened for half a minute, a frown gathering on his brow as he looked casually around. A crowd of Indo-Chinese, the men with clerical collars, the women wearing nuns' habits, twittered past the booth, but the other phones remained unoccupied.

"That is not good," he said when Treynet had finished speaking. "It is very bad. Steps must at once be taken. This snooper must be—What! Did you say Bolan?"

The hand holding the receiver shook. "But he must be suppressed at once. I would prefer it if he could be taken alive and kept for me. There are certain differences between Mr. Bolan and myself that remain to be resolved. But, if necessary, shoot him down on sight."

Another pause, and then, "Not from this end, no. I cannot imagine why such a person...especially in his present international status...Well, you must do what you think best. But soon."

Second coin clunked into the box, leaving two on view.

Schmitt-Heinkel said, "The merchandise should be with you tomorrow. Allow four days for refining. The big distribution should be possible Thursday of next week. Can you organize the rally for that day? You can? Excellent.''

Treynet talked some more. A third coin dropped. Finally the German said, ''Good, good. All is under control. As for Bolan, I have ideas. You had better put Lange on the line.''

Schmitt-Heinkel talked rapidly in a low voice for several minutes. The last coin fell. When the red light above the hook blinked, indicating that the paid time had elapsed, he said, ''Very well, Lange. Be sure that you do. Alive if you can. Report to me personally by Saturday at the latest. You know my hotel suite.''

He replaced the handset and walked away.

He took the elevator down to the departure level, where it was less crowded, and looked for a men's room. There were several. Schmitt-Heinkel was not satisfied until he found one with only two travelers visible. They were drying their hands on a hot-air blower above the washbasins, and it was evident they were about to leave. He went into one of the cubicles and locked the door.

His subsequent behavior was curious. He stripped off his outer clothes, dislodged the uncomfortable rubber pads that had puffed his cheeks into jowls, then removed a white wig.

From the valise he took a suit of a coarser material and more conservative cut, round-toed black shoes, a small mirror, spirit gum and false hair. He unstrapped the body cushion that had lent him his bulky shape and packed it, along with the remainder of Doktor Dieter Schmitt-Heinkel, into the holdall.

Ten minutes later he walked out into the empty washroom—a compactly built middle-aged man wearing steel-rimmed spectacles, with a bushy mustache below iron-gray hair cut short in the eastern-European fashion. He took the shuttle bus to Orly Airport on the other side of Paris.

There, still carrying the holdall, he checked in at a French domestic airline desk, tourist class, one piece of cabin baggage only.

8

Mack Bolan's Paris hotel was on the rue St. Augustin, not far from the Opera. It was a small, narrow building with a slanted glass canopy fanning out over the entrance. The rash of touring-club recommendations displayed on either side of the doors made it a natural enough voice for Bolan in his role of vacationer. More important was the fact that there was a fire exit leading to an alleyway that ran through to a wide avenue.

And that from the bathroom window of his sixth-floor room it was an easy drop to a flat roof from which an agile man could reach the emergency stairway outside an apartment house on the rue de Richelieu.

Even holed up between battles, Bolan liked to keep his options open.

On Thursday evening he returned to the hotel after dark feeling tired and irritable. He had spent an unprofitable day sorting through a mountain of press cuttings in the morgue of the newspaper where the columnist killed by the car bomb had worked. Over lunch that day, the newspaperman had promised to fill him in on the more scandalous aspects of Treynet, father and son.

The explosion had put an end to that. The bulky files of clippings, which went back as far as the thirties, told him little more than he could have learned from any French Winchell or Hopper. In particular, there was no mention or reference, however small, to any kind of eagle's nest.

Bolan was wondering where the hell to start next as he thrust the key into the lock of his room.

The door swung open at his touch.

He froze, staring through the widening space.

A young woman was slumped in an armchair between the night table and the window, the street lighting that pierced the slats of the venetian blind barring her face with black shadows.

At first he thought she was sleeping, but a bloodshot eye opened between two dark stripes and in a low, hoarse voice she croaked the single word, "Bolan?"

The Executioner swore softly. How many more strangers knew his real name?

One hand flashed toward the left lapel beneath which the Beretta was snugly holstered. At the same time he swept his free hand across the light switch, leaped through the gap in the doorway, and flattened himself against the wall.

He was in no danger from this visitor.

She couldn't have been more than sixteen or seventeen, but she was a pathetic sight: a haggard, bloodless face, lank, shoulder-length hair that looked as though it had not been washed in weeks, dark circles beneath the eyes. She was wearing scuffed blue jeans, dirty white tennis shoes and a ragged shirt that did nothing to hide the fact that she wore no brassiere.

"Who are you?" Bolan demanded.

She appeared too exhausted to raise her heavy lids. "Eliane sent me," she said dully.

"I don't know any Eliane." He closed the door, strode abruptly across the room and pulled back the unbuttoned sleeve of her shirt. On the matchstick arm were three grimy strips of plaster and a score of small red scars, some of them angry and inflamed.

Bolan shook his head sadly. "What do you want with me?"

The girl's cracked lips trembled. "I want out," she said.

Bolan's voice was severe. "What are you into, anyway? Heroin and the JETs? Is that it?"

She nodded miserably.

He choked back the words he would like to have spoken, words that would have expressed his contempt and loathing for the vileness spawned by scum like the Treynets. "The state you're in," he said more kindly, "you'd have to be dried out professionally. In a clinic. Maybe a psychiatric ward. Why come to me? And how come suddenly you want out?"

She was crying now, the wasted body racked with harsh sobs. "B-b-because of Raoul," she wept. "I w-w-wanted to get my own b-back. I wanted them to suffer, too. It was because of them that he...that he died. It was like they killed my Raoul."

"Who's Raoul?"

"My friend. The only friend I had left in the w-w-world. I...that is, we...we might have been...all right. Only they made him...It was, I don't know, two or three days ago. They m-made him plant a bomb in a car. Here in Paris."

"I know about the bomb," Bolan said grimly.

"But s-s-something went wrong. It went off too soon. Raoul was on the bike but he c-c-couldn't get away in t-time. He was...he was..." The rest of her words were drowned in a fresh outburst of sobbing.

Yeah, the bike. That was it. Bolan recalled lifting the mangled remains of a powerful machine off the body of a woman in that devastated street. And something heaving in the center of the roadway that he preferred to forget.

There was no point telling this ravaged child what he thought of youths weak or vicious enough to be ordered or blackmailed into terrorist action. He said brusquely, "Okay. Your boyfriend got himself zapped. But why come to me? How did you know my name, where I was?"

"Eliane sent me. I told you."

"And *I* told *you* I don't know any Eliane."

"You do, you do." The swollen lids lifted. Eyes still brimming with tears stared at him. "Well, anyway, she knows you all right. J.E.'s broad at the château. The classy blonde, Eliane Falcoz."

Bolan caught his breath. Of course! The girl in the flowered dress who had warned him to quit the estate and tipped him off to the Lambretta scooter. Okay, that he could understand. But how did *she* know who he was? Why send this pathetic kid to him? And how did she know where to send her?

Damn, Bolan thought once more, was the entire population of Europe wise to his movements?

"What is your name?" he queried.

"Chantal."

"Look, Chantal, I'm asking you again, why should Eliane Falcoz send you to me? I can't help you kick the habit."

"It's not that." The girl's upper lip was twitching. She scratched her left forearm. "She thought you might help me pay them back."

"Who? Treynet's gang? I don't see—"

"And she thought I might be able to help you."

Bolan lowered himself into a chair, hitched it nearer to her. "Oh yeah?" he said quietly. "And how would you do that?"

"I can tell you how they work," Chantal said.

"I know how the JETs work. They get spaced-out kids like your buddy and encourage them to plant bombs or shoot folks down in aid of whatever crackpot fantasies they have. And when they've made enough trouble for enough people and ordinary folks start taking the law into their own hands, lynching suspected terrorists, the JETs step in, seize power and say, look what we saved you from."

"That's only a part of it." For the first time the girl showed some animation. "I wasn't always an addict," she said defiantly. "I was a sociology student at the Sorbonne before I...before they..."

"Before you were hooked. Okay."

"You don't understand the scope of their organization. They're using dope to suborn our whole generation."

Bolan's brows were raised. "You mean—?"

"Shooting parties, snorting, smoking, group sex, perversions, anything. Forget the violence for a moment. That's just the frosting on the cake. For them the drug scene's the big thing. That's going to be their lever."

"You mean the classic technique? Get you all hooked, then up the price each time you need a fix? Fill the political party coffers that way until suddenly the price is so far out of sight that you can't make it. and then you'll do anything, anything—like planting a bomb, for instance—to get that fix. That way they rake in the dough for starters and have themselves an endless supply of slaves later who'll stoop to any filth they tell them to. Isn't that the scenario?"

"No!" the girl cried passionately. "No! You don't understand, you see. They *lower* the price each time. Until they're practically giving it away."

"They make it *cheaper*?" Bolan was incredulous. As far as he knew this was running counter to all the precepts of the Mafia. Jacking up the price was at the base of all their callous thinking.

"They buy the stuff in bulk and refine it themselves," Chantal said. "Don't you see? It's voters they want, not slaves."

Bolan stared at her.

"By the time we're of voting age," she explained, "we're going to be totally dependent. But totally. So then the message is, vote for us..or no more dope. And you know who's going to vote for who. This way, when the whole scene blows up as you say it will—as they intend it to, right?—they don't have to *seize* power, they can say they were democratically voted in. And it'll be true. That's why the cut-rate shit. The easier they make it for us to stay hooked, the more votes they get in the end."

The Executioner whistled. So that was it. Brognola's intel had been heading the right way, but it didn't go far enough. It was a bigger deal than he'd thought.

It wasn't just that the JETs were orchestrating those terrorist outrages; the outrages themselves were part of a more ambitious plan that was already operating on a national scale.

Not only was it a bigger deal than Brognola had thought, it was going to be a tougher battle than Bolan had bargained for.

But before he could come out from undercover and go into action he had to have more information. He knew now just how the tentacles of this particular Hydra gripped, but he needed to locate the head before he could start slashing.

"Chantal," he said urgently, "listen to me. Maybe I can help you at that. I have contacts and I'll sure try, I promise you. Your friend Raoul will be avenged. But first I have to know more about the JETs. We know what they do and how they operate, but it's the details that I lack. I need times, dates, places...especially places. That's where you have to help. Will you do that for me? For Raoul?"

She was scratching her arm again. From time to time the frail body was seized by a fit of shuddering. "I need a fix," she muttered. "I've been here longer than I—"

"Listen!" Bolan rapped again. "You've got to help. You're the only one on the inside. Will you try?"

She nodded in a dispirited way. "Oh, sure. Look, I have to get back to my—"

"Okay, okay, go get your fix. But tell me one thing first. What or where is the Eagle's Nest?"

The head shook slowly from side to side, lank hair swinging. "I heard of it. I heard them talking. But I don't know." She began to struggle to her feet. "Look, mister, I have to split."

Bolan grabbed her thin shoulders. "But tell me first. The Eagle's Nest. Can you find out?" He shook her. "It's important. For you, as well as Raoul. Will you try?"

Shivering, she looked up suddenly, a gleam of intelligence returning to her hollow eyes. "I guess so. I think I could. Give me a couple of hours, and I'll see what I can dig up...." All at once, she dissolved into tears. "I have to go!" she shouted.

Bolan stood up. "You need bread?"

Again she shook her head. "I'm loaded with the stuff, but it's back at my place, and it'll take me half an hour!" She moved toward the door.

"Where can I contact you? When will you know?"

"Know?"

"The Eagle's Nest," Bolan repeated, trying to master his impatience. "When you've found out."

"Oh. Yeah. Sure." She shook herself like a dog coming out of the sea. "Look, you'd best come by my pad. Say around midnight, one o'clock."

"Okay. What's the address?"

"It's on the rue St. Véran. One-two-seven. It's kind of a commune. You know. Anything I have, you can pick it up then."

"I'll be there." Bolan thrust a couple of bills into her slack hand. "Take the side entrance," he said. "Go through to the avenue. There's a line of cabs there. It'll be quicker than the Metro."

At the door she turned, and for the first time a wan smile cracked open her wasted features. "You're nice," she said. "I'll do what I can."

When she had gone Bolan shook his head. Pity, disgust and a cold, implacable fury against the scum who could deliberately reduce human beings to this level struggled to come uppermost in his mind. He punched his right fist fiercely into the palm of his left hand.

This was one he had to win.

If there are already kids like Chantal all over France today, he thought, God knows what hell could break loose tomorrow.

Live Now, Pay Later. They used to say that was the motto of the consumer society.

Live Hard was Bolan's creed.

If he had his way, the gutter rats behind the JETs were going to pay now, so that kids like Chantal could live later.

And longer.

9

The rue St. Véran ran through a neighborhood known locally as "the Islet"—an enclave of urban wasteland that lay between a railroad terminus and a tangle of freight yards and abandoned factories just inside the ring road encircling the inner city.

It was an area of gutted nineteenth-century apartment houses, boarded-up stores and vacant lots littered with bricks, tires and the rusted wrecks of delivery trucks. Certain dead-end streets—the Impasse Chalon, the Passage Brunoy—were unsafe to walk alone. In its atmosphere of desolation and decay the place reminded Bolan of the worst part of the South Bronx.

He drove the length of the street, past shored-up walls daubed with graffiti, past grimed shards of glass that still clung to the window frames of long-gone workshops. The public phone booths had been vandalized and most of the streetlamps smashed. His headlights swept over curbside rows of battered automobiles, many jacked up on bricks, some with hoods, doors or even engines missing.

He had replaced the Peugeot's shattered glasswork, but the car still boasted a punctured trunk and a crumpled front fender. Even so, parking the sedan here and leaving it unattended, he knew, would lose the Hertz company their third rental car in less than a week. Ten minutes later, and he'd be lucky to find that only the wheels and the radio had been stolen.

He decided to leave it in an underground parking lot nearer the eastern expressway out of the city and return to the area on foot. The all-night lot was automated, the kind where you took a ticket to raise the entrance barrier, and then fed coins into a machine that punched the card so that it would lift an exit gate when you wanted to leave.

There were three levels. Bolan drove down the ramp to the first. Now—it was ten after midnight—almost all of the white-lined parking slots were vacant. Only occasionally a dull gleam on a curve of metal beneath the dim lighting betrayed the presence of a car left overnight in the cavernous gloom.

He left the Peugeot beside one of the square stone pillars supporting the roof and switched off engine and lights.

The pillar saved his life.

The two gunmen opened fire as he was getting out of the car. But he bent forward slightly and found himself protected temporarily behind the stonework.

Glass from the Peugeot's window smashed and bullets splatted against the post almost before his mind registered the sound of the gunshots, deafening in the confined space. His cheek was stung by chips of stone.

Bolan was flat on the cement floor beneath the Peugeot, the stainless-steel AutoMag clasped in both hands, waiting for an identifiable target.

The guns roared again. It was heavy-caliber stuff, he reckoned. The car rocked as slugs punched the bodywork just above his head. One ricocheted off the center of a wheel and whined shrilly into the distance.

He knew where they were firing from now, over the hood of a heavy sedan parked on the far side of the aisle that led to the exit ramp. Before he hit back and revealed his exact position, he wanted to check out the terrain. Shifting his position slightly, he edged forward and peered out beneath the Peugeot's front bumper.

Halfway along the aisle, he saw a concrete stairway leading up to street level. Bolan had three choices: the entrance ramp, the exit ramp, or the stairway. They'd expect him to take the last, so he'd make for the first.

Big Thunder bellowed, bucking in his hands as he loosed two probing rounds at the big sedan. Glass shattered and fell.

He heard a scrape of feet. They were separating, hoping to enfilade him. Two shots angled in beneath the front wheels of the Peugeot, furrowing the floor. But Bolan was already upright and behind the pillar.

He stooped, reaching for a fragment of cement gouged out by one of the heavy slugs. If they were anticipating a dash for the stairway, they would be watching the space between the car and the next column on his right, waiting for him to try and cross the aisle. He lobbed the fragment that way, rattling it into a bar of shadow cast by the pillar.

The hoods fired.

But Bolan had gone the other way. He dodged behind the Peugeot and then, with the gunners facing in the wrong direction, risked a sprint to the far side of the aisle. He was now in the same row, shielded from them only by the bulk of the sedan.

Behind him there was a panel truck. He dropped to his hands and knees, crawling beneath it.

Big Thunder was in his right hand; the silenced Beretta, unleathered from its shoulder rig, was in his left. The stun grenades had been left at the vacation camp, but in such a confined space he would not have dared use them anyway; the effect would have been as dangerous for him as for the enemy.

Bolan's strategy was to draw the fire of the ambushers until they needed to reload and then, as they slammed in fresh clips or box magazines, make a break for the entrance ramp. It relied on two unknowns: their rate of fire and the guns they were using.

What the hell. Chances were there to be taken.

From beneath the truck he could make out shadowy movement on the far side of the sedan. As he had thought, there were just two of them. In the reflected light he could make out a foot and the lower part of a leg that was not masked by one of the big car's wheels.

Aiming carefully, he held his breath and squeezed the trigger of the AutoMag.

The thunderous report was joined by a howl of pain. Something heavy lurched against metal and then clattered to the ground. The space beneath the sedan was now partly obscured by a recumbent form.

Bolan fired again and the body jerked.

The second man knew now where the deadly fire was coming from. Sheltered by the front wheel, fender and hood, he hosed three shots onto the floor beside the truck, aiming to bounce them up and wing the unseen marksman.

Five plus three made eight, and Bolan was already up and running for the ramp.

He sped across the empty slots between pillars, hoping to keep the stonework between him and the remaining hood.

But the guy must have moved out wide, silhouetting him against the dimly lit slope. He'd picked up his buddy's iron—and those were no 8-shot clips—now the underground lot echoed to a regular fusilade.

Each time the muzzle flashes stabbed the dark, a giant shadow leaped ahead of the speeding Executioner and swept across the ceiling. One of the slugs passed so close to his head that he felt the disturbance of air on the lobe of his ear.

Bolan leaped behind the nearest pillar.

The ramp was still fifty feet away. Should he move back toward the central stairway where several cars in the farther row offered cover, and try to take the killer out?

Before he could make up his mind, a starter whirred. An engine burst into life. Dazzling headlamp beams lanced the gloom, and the big sedan moved slowly out into the aisle.

Bolan had guessed right. The killers had been sheltering behind their own car.

The lights swung toward the ramp, throwing into brilliant relief every detail of the aisle and the pillars lining it.

Bolan ducked back behind the one sheltering him. He glanced swiftly over his shoulder at the ramp.

A small car was rolling silently down the slope.

A godsend? Another late-night driver looking for parking space, a witness before whom the gunman dare risk nothing more? Or was this, too, part of the ambush—a reinforcement perhaps called up by radio?

The question was soon answered.

The sedan was a large American-style automobile. A Chevy? An Olds? A ten-year-old Lincoln? On the wrong side of the lights it was impossible to tell. But it was in any case an unwieldy car.

The one on the ramp, however, was something else. An extremely maneuverable French minicar, a Renault R-5. And as soon as the sedan was in position, it began zigzagging speedily between the pillars on either side of the aisle, light beams searching out the hunted man.

Simultaneously the sedan advanced at a snail's pace, the headlamps weaving slowly from side to side as the driver eased the wheel left, then right.

Bolan backed off to avoid being picked out by the powerful beams, then jumped hastily around to the far side of the pillar as the Renault swung his way.

But soon the two cars would draw level, one on either side of his refuge. Then he would be pinned as effectively as a moth on a display board, with the four faces of the pillar all bathed in merciless light.

Okay, so the best means of defense is attack. How often had he drummed that ancient rule into his men in Vietnam and after?

He waited until the R-5's lights wheeled away, then stepped calmly out from behind the pillar and shot out the sedan's lights with the Beretta. Before the guy behind the wheel had time to recover from his surprise and return his fire, Bolan was back behind the stonework and racing for the group of cars parked in the far row.

Because the Beretta was silenced, the man behind the wheel of the Renault was equally taken unawares. Tires screeched as he finally wrenched the minicar around to intercept his quarry. Shots rang out from both cars. A slug struck the floor by Bolan's feet and whined off into the distance. Somebody shouted something in a language he couldn't identify.

Then light brightened around the edges of the nearest pillar. The Renault was dangerously near. So was the lampless sedan. They were trying to bracket him.

Bolan dashed for the nearest parked vehicles. He hurled himself sideways as flames belched from the open windows of the pursuers' cars. But now he knew what he needed to know.

There were only two guns, one in each car.

Panting, he crouched down behind a small convertible sports model. Tires squealed again as the Renault accelerated, circled around, and then skidded to a halt facing the convertible.

There was a steering lock on the little car, but it was no problem to reach a hand through the canvas flap beneath the driver's window and ease off the hand brake. Bracing one foot against the back wall, Bolan shoved with all his strength.

The convertible rolled slowly toward the Renault.

The hoods imagined Bolan was using it as a shield, a barrier to advance behind, and opened fire from both sides. But he was standing by the wall in a bar of shadow between two of the overhead lights.

Without the headlamp dazzle, the gun flashes just above the sedan's door made a perfect target. He aimed six inches above them and punched out three rounds from the AutoMag.

The dim shape behind the sedan's wheel vanished backward. A gun dropped to the ground outside the door. In the reflected light from the R-5's headlamps, a fan of crimson stained the inside of the sedan's windshield and then slowly subsided.

Two down and one to go.

The Renault swerved around the empty, coasting convertible and approached the wall at an angle. The driver was steering with one hand, his gun arm dangling on the outside of the door, ready to come up and shoot.

Bolan doubled back, turned at right angles as the headlamp beams caught up with him...and leaped as the killer opened fire.

He landed on the hood of another parked sedan, scrambled to the roof and whirled around as the driver leaned sideways to peer up and get a better shot at him.

This time it was the Beretta that transmitted the Executioner's message of death. Firing down through the Renault's windshield, he shattered the glass and stitched the hardman to his seat with needles of lead.

The Renault ran slowly on and crunched to a halt against the wall when the motor stalled.

Bolan jumped down and ran to the guy he had shot in the leg. Big Thunder's second round had delivered the kayo. The softnose slug had smacked the punk in the nape of the neck and almost taken his head from his body. He lay in a pool of red that was already congealing.

Bolan pushed the holed convertible back to its original position, drove the sedan down to face the wall and left the Renault where it was. He opened the lid of the sedan's huge trunk—it was a Ford Galaxy, he saw now that he had time to look—and stuffed all three bodies inside. He might need to use the Peugeot again, and there was no point leaving the lot untidy and attracting the attention of the law just yet. Automated as it was, the place would function without the benefit of personnel until six-thirty the following morning.

Bolan left the guns with their late owners. He reloaded and releathered his own artillery, walked up the stairway to street level and headed for rue St. Véran.

On foot, the desolation was even more evident. The neighborhood, which had teemed with Oriental delicatessen and Chinese restaurants before Chinese food became fashionable, was slated for total demolition to make way for some new development. In the meantime, it remained a festering sore on the face of the city, its buildings condemned and their inhabitants evacuated.

Squatters—vagrants, junkies, winos, the derelicts of a society that didn't give a damn—had invaded the decrepit buildings and found shelter there. Picking his way across weed-infested vacant lots, Bolan saw tin-roof shacks walled with oil drums and plastic, fires fueled with wood torn from staircases and doors, candlelight flickering behind glassless windows.

A tall, red brick ruin, 127, rue St. Véran, stood between a roofless schoolhouse and a rubble-strewn space that had once been a playground. Grass grew in the cracks between the uneven flagstones paving the sidewalk outside.

Inside, demolition crews had torn out stairs and destroyed much of the flooring, but like most tenements the block was crisscrossed at the rear with a zigzag of fire escapes, and the floating population had used these to move into whatever space remained.

Unshaven youths sprawled over the lowest flight of the rusted iron laddering. They wore ragged clothes and they smelled unwashed, but they were listening to hard rock that blared from a huge twin-speaker stereo radio that looked brand-new. A four-foot pullout aerial gleamed silver in the light reflected from one of the surviving streetlamps fifty yards away.

Bolan approached the group, scenting the odor of marijuana. "Where can I find Chantal's pad?" he asked.

They'd certainly seen him coming, but nobody replied and none of them even looked up.

He repeated the question, raising his voice to make himself heard over the jangle and thump of the music. One of the punks glanced up and then spit through the railings, but still nobody answered.

Bolan compressed his lips. He strode up to the foot of the stairway, leaned over and stabbed one finger down on the radio's Stop button. In the sudden silence he said, "I asked you a question."

The heaviest of the youths—he was about twenty years old, with long sideburns and dangerous eyes—was squatting by the radio. He switched the music on again and stood up. "We don't go too strong on strangers around here," he said. "Especially strangers who bust in unasked and mess with our property."

"I asked you a civil question," Bolan repeated.

"Fuck your question. What are you, some kind of a bastard cop?" Standing on the third step, the boy was a head taller than Bolan. He raised a cigarette to his mouth, sucked in smoke and air, then passed the joint to a ferret-faced punk on the other side of the radio. The punk took a drag and stood up.

"Hey, that's a real nice coat asshole's wearin' there," he said, blowing out smoke. He passed the joint to a third boy.

"Yeah," the heavy youth drawled. "Real nice. I wouldn't mind havin' me a coat like that." He reached out and fingered the tweed lapel. "You figure out any way I could get me one, Louis?"

The third punk grinned. He breathed out smoke he had been holding low down in his lungs. "I'll sure try," he said.

They were each standing up now, five of them in all. The two who hadn't spoken yet guffawed. "Maybe we could see if this jerk's got balls beneath that coat," one of them said.

Bolan decided to finish it. Ferretface had picked up a piece of wood with rusty nails sticking through the end, and Louis now held a knife in his fist.

Bolan flung his arms up and outward, knocking the hand away from his coat. He seized the heavy punk's ears, tangling his fingers in the long greasy hair, and jerked the head sharply downward...down to smash against his own hard forehead.

As the guy yelled in pain and surprise, Bolan released him, drove an elbow backward into the guts of one of the nameless punks, then kicked the knife from Louis's hand.

Ferretface's wooden baton was swinging toward Bolan's head. He ducked, grabbed the hand holding the club, and jerked. Ferretface flew over his shoulder and landed on his back with a thump that knocked the breath from his body.

Bolan stepped in and hit Louis twice; one left, one right; one to the jaw, one over the heart. The boy dropped like a felled tree. The punk who had been elbowed was sitting on the ground trying to choke breath back into his lungs. The second nameless one was running. That left only the heavy one.

He was swaying on the lowest stair, one hand held over his face. Blood trickled through the fingers from his smashed nose. But the other hand was drawing a length of lead piping wrapped in leather from his hip pocket.

Bolan kicked him in the crotch. He kicked the fallen pipe out of the way as the youth went down screeching, then he walked to where Ferretface lay on his back.

The Executioner stooped down, bunched the front of the boy's jacket in his left fist and lifted him to his feet. He picked him off the ground and held him with feet dangling at the full stretch of his arm. "Maybe you forgot," he said, "I asked you a question. How can I find Chantal's pad?"

The boy's face blanched in terror. In the faint light Bolan could see his eyes flick right and then left. "I don't know any Chantal," he stammered.

"Thin girl. Sixteen, seventeen. Long hair. Heavily into horse, I'd say. Raoul's girl."

"I don't know any Raoul, neither."

"With the JETs. Wrote himself out of the script in that car-bomb deal."

"I tell you I don't know any—"

The boy broke off with a scream as Bolan, still holding him off the ground, began slapping his face hard with his free hand. "You're going to tell me," Bolan panted, "where I can find Chantal."

"All right," Ferretface shouted. "All *right*, for fuck's sake! You don't have to get aggressive."

Bolan put him down. "Well?" he said quietly.

"Next staircase along," the boy said sullenly. "The attic floor."

Bolan turned to look at the quartet of decimated punks, opening his coat to show Big Thunder holstered on his hip. "I don't know how long I shall be up there," he said, "but if I see one of you bums within two hundred yards when I come down, I'll shoot you."

He swung around and walked to the next stairway.

It was a long climb to the attic floor. The top passageway stank of urine, rotten fruit and dirty linen. There was a light showing beneath an ill-fitting door. Bolan knocked and went in.

The room was a disaster. Soiled clothes lay in untidy heaps beneath the posters that covered the walls. There was a photo blowup of German troops marching down the Champs-Elysées tacked over the empty window embrasure. Rusty water dripped into a cracked washbasin, and piles of hardcover books tied with string littered the floor.

The only furniture in the room was a sagging divan.

Chantal lay facedown on the mattress in a tangle of gray sheets, one thin arm trailing the floor. She had been dead, Bolan estimated, for more than an hour.

OD'd, of course. Syringe, spoon and empty sachet were scattered conveniently near the limp hand; a candle still sent a lean flame up into the stale air.

But the overdose had been forcibly administered, for sure. Evenly spaced bruises on the girl's upper arms and thighs showed where the clamped fingers of the murderers had held her down. Red marks left by the gag ran from the corners of her mouth.

The kid had kept her word just the same.

After they had gone, she had survived long enough, had marshaled her failing senses sufficiently, to leave Bolan a message.

Roughly scrawled in lipstick on the dusty floorboards beside the bed were the letters *E* and *N*.

And beneath them, nearer the lifeless hand, in smudged eyeliner that was barely legible, the phrase, *s-heinke chemcl manu com*.

Bolan memorized the whole cryptic message. Then he picked up a dirty T-shirt, damped it beneath the faucet and obliterated the lettering, savagely scrubbing at the characters until they had become a meaningless smear.

He left the room and closed the door. No one bothered Bolan as he hurried down the fire escape. He went in search of a usable phone booth so that he could phone the police and report a murder.

10

Bolan did not sleep that night. His rage and grief at the callous slaughter of Chantal demanded action, any kind of action so long as it was immediate. The pathetic child had come to him for help, had died because she had come and because *she* had offered to help *him*.

Okay, the killers would pay.

But first they had to be identified. And he had to know where to hit them.

That they were part of the Treynet setup was certain. But which part?

Bolan figured the best way to avenge the girl and simultaneously advance from the present stalemate was to follow up her dying message.

The letters *E* and *N* had to stand for Eagle's Nest, because that was what he had asked her. And he was convinced that this was the key to the JETs' organization.

The words beneath were less easy to interpret. It seemed clear enough that *chemcl manu com* was the nearest her failing strength could make to "chemical manufacturing company."

And so?

So what the hell could *s-heinke* mean?

An abbreviation of the company's name? Some kind of instruction, some misspelled clue for Bolan himself? A warning?

The first bet seemed the best, if only because he could make nothing coherent of the syllables any other way. Also, checking out a name was something he could start right now, at three o'clock in the morning.

He went to the all-night post office on the rue du Louvre and asked for the city telephone directories.

He was pretty sure he had been followed back from the parking lot after he had made his anonymous call to the police and collected the Peugeot. But he could not be certain. There is always traffic in nighttime Paris—taxis, patrol cars, street sweepers, newspaper-delivery trucks, early bread vans, nightclubbers driving home, smart little sports cars expertly handled by the whores who hustle from them.

In such conditions on a short journey it would be difficult enough to spot a tail if you were looking through the rear window of a cab, practically impossible if you had to concentrate on your own driving.

Just the same, Bolan was sure he had been followed.

So what? He would deal with an attack if and when it came.

Bolan pored over the seventy-nine-page *H* section in the two-volume Paris telephone directory. Nothing. Maybe he'd got it wrong. He sighed and turned to the pages listing names beginning with *S*. Still nothing.

Bolan rubbed his eyes. His head was aching with so much concentration on small print. The gray light of dawn was seeping through the post-office windows. Outside in the street he could hear the shouts of garbage men and the clatter of trash cans.

He closed the book and stood up. What he needed was an alphabetical listing of some kind that covered the whole country.

The idea came to him when he was swallowing a large black coffee in an early-opening brasserie across the street from the post office.

Dumbbell, he thought. If the organization was incorporated—what the British called a limited liability company and the French a *société anonymée*—it would by law have to be registered. If it was a public company with stock quoted on the bourse, it would also be obliged to disclose the names of its directors.

Somewhere in Paris there must be an official, centralized register of companies. And its contents must be available from the data banks of some computer someplace.

There was and they were.

The newspaper whose morgue he had consulted gave him the information he wanted. At ten o'clock Bolan presented himself at an annex to the Ministry of the Interior on the rue de Rivoli, opposite the Louvre-Concorde Hotel, just across the street from the Palais Royal and the Comédie-Française.

The register was open to public inspection. And as he had hoped, it was alphabetical countrywide.

Bolan asked to see printouts for certain sectors of the *H* and *S* series.

There were a hell of a lot. It still took him more than an hour. But at last he struck pay dirt.

He had, in fact, been on the wrong track. The *S* was not an initial; the next symbol was not a *C*. It was what it seemed to be: a dash or hyphen. The name was double-barreled, even if Chantal had only managed to achieve the first letter of the first part.

S-H. Bolan found the full reference in the seventh column he checked: Schmitt-Heinkel SA, Manufacturers of Chemical Supplies.

The registered offices, together with the company's factory, were at La Trinité-en-Royans, a village in the Vercors, southwest of Grenoble.

That didn't tell Bolan much. He knew the Vercors was a limestone massif on the fringes of the Alps. He had never heard of La Trinité. The names of the company's board of directors meant nothing to him. But a cross-reference beneath the entry told him everything.

A subsidiary company, listed as distributor of the manufacturer's products, was known as Eagle Chemicals.

The President of Eagle Chemicals was one Jules Treynet.

Bolan expelled his breath in a long sigh of relief. No doubt now where the mysterious Eagle's Nest was. A place in the mountains known as the Vercors.

He was more convinced than ever now that it must be the nerve center of all the Treynet operations. Would it actually be at the factory? Or was there another kind of HQ in or near the village of La Trinité? Was the factory itself a cover, a regular operation, or was it just a blind?

There was, of course, only one way to find out.

Go there. Yeah, advance on the target with all guns blazing. Crack the son of a bitch wide open before the guys inside knew what hit them.

But first a recon. In depth.

There was an airfield at Grenoble. From a phone booth on the rue de Rivoli he called his hotel and asked them to reserve a seat for him on the next available plane. And a hotel room in the city.

Bolan left the kiosk and started across the street toward the colonnades on the far side. He stood on a central pedestrian refuge, waiting for a flood of traffic released by a green light to pass. It was then that the bikers made their play.

They had hung in behind the fast-moving phalanx of cars and cabs and delivery trucks, only approaching as Bolan, thinking the coast was now clear, stepped out on the second half of the crossing.

He paused in midstride, wondering if they were going to brake, ride in front of him or swerve behind him if he increased his pace.

They did none of those things.

What they did do took him completely by surprise. An attack in broad daylight in the center of Paris never occurred to him.

The maneuver was expertly carried out.

There were four of them—black leather, black boots, silver visored helmets. They passed near Bolan, two in front and two behind, and then slowed to walking speed, closing in until they were riding two abreast, in two pairs, the handlebars of each pair almost touching. The front couple were less than six inches ahead of the other two.

Bolan was boxed in between the four sets of handlebars.

It was crazy. In the narrow space walled by the rear wheels of the leading pair and the front wheels of the two bikes behind, he was imprisoned as effectively as a bird in a cage.

From in front, two black-gloved hands seized his upper arms in a viselike grip. At the same time something hard dug into the small of his back. One of the guys behind had a gun on him.

Before he realized what was happening, Bolan was being propelled along, hedged in by the riders.

In a flash he reviewed the options open to him.

It was too chancy, attempting a vault over the machines on either side; he could trip, he could pull machine and rider down on himself, he would risk a slug in the spine. The bikers looked too tough to let him get away with a back somersault over the rear handlebars, and if he dove across the front pair he'd still be playing hare with the hounds behind him.

Gradually the bikes were accelerating, forcing him to go along with them, the grip on his arms tightening. Bolan went from a walk to a trot to a run, sprinting now so fast that he could keep standing only by a supreme effort.

They were approaching the place de la Concorde. He could see at once what the hardmen had in mind. Among the wedges of parked cars and sightseers' coaches islanding the huge square, they could speedily dispose of him unseen by drivers traversing the traffic lanes that crossed the place.

He had to get out, fast, before they hustled him that far.

Bolan went the only way open to him, the one way they would not expect.

Down.

He pitched forward, broke the grip on his arms, plummeted facedown to the pavement.

The wheels hissed close on either side of him. He heard a yell, a thin squeal of disk brakes, a scrape of rubber as the bikers wheeled around. But by then he was on his feet and running for the last block of colonnades before the square.

They wouldn't be crazy enough to give chase among the crowds of prelunch shoppers in one of the ritziest streets in Paris. Not even if they were junkies as well as JETs.

Bolan was wrong.

Women screamed and men shouted as the four bikes swung up onto the vaulted sidewalk and roared in pursuit.

Bolan dodged behind a stone pillar, the Beretta now in his right hand. He didn't know what to do. In open country or deserted alleys he would gladly have taken on the four men. But here among the crowd? If he opened fire, there was a chance that the bikers would use innocent bystanders as shields. That was the classic terrorist ploy.

But if he went on running, weaving right and left, and the killers opened fire, those innocent folks risked getting mowed down by the assassins' bullets. To run straight, on the other hand, was to invite a quick death.

He did not have to make the decision.

The crowd had scattered but not fast enough. The four helmeted hoods rode them down. An elderly woman fell, dropping a paper sack that burst open and cascaded fruit and vegetables across the sidewalk and onto the roadway. A man lurched backward through a plate-glass window.

For a split second one of the riders was unmarked, clear of the milling crowd, fifty feet away from the Executioner. The Beretta coughed three times. The rider's visor starred, blood dribbled beneath the lower rim of the crash helmet, and he fell forward and sideways, taking the machine with him.

One of the others had wheeled back onto the road among a fresh flow of traffic. Bolan had to run or he would be taken on his flank. He couldn't fire again; there were still people between him and the remaining two motorcyclists.

He turned and ran for the corner of the rue St. Florentin at the end of the block.

The two bikers on the sidewalk opened fire as they rode.

Each of them held, one-handed, an Ingram MAC-11, the world's lightest, shortest, deadliest machine pistol. The MAC-11's 30-round magazine is charged with .45-parabellum rounds. And the little gun, which fires at the astonishing rate of 1,200 rounds per minute, is fitted with the world's most efficient "sound suppressor."

The sudden, silenced hail of death transformed the colonnade into a slaughterhouse.

Callously sprayed right and left, the heavy slugs wreaked havoc with the already panic-stricken crowd.

By some miracle Bolan was untouched. He dashed around the corner onto the rue St. Florentin, as much to save further massacres beneath the colonnades as to escape the killers' bullets.

By the curb a sleek green sports car was waiting. From the futuristic body a gull-wing door opened upward. An urgent voice called, "Bolan! Get in!"

Instinctively he obeyed. He stooped and sank into the luxurious leather seat as the exhaust snarled and the car shot away. Panting, he reached up and pulled the door shut, looked sideways at his rescuer. A blond girl wearing cream-colored jeans and a turquoise silk shirt.

Eliane Falcoz.

Right then Bolan had too many unanswered questions to do more than stare. In any case the scenario left little room for speech.

The rue St. Florentin is one-way, leaving the rue de Rivoli. The girl wrenched the car around in a U-turn against the traffic flow, rocketed back between the vehicles speeding along Rivoli, and then tweaked the wheel to create a havoc of angry horns and stomped brakes on the place de la Concorde. From there she turned right and accelerated up the long slope of the Champs-Elysées.

Bolan allowed his breath to escape and glanced around him.

The car was a Lamborghini LP-500 Countach in top tune. Eighty thousand dollars worth of custom-built, midengined projectile pushing out 425 horsepower that gave a maximum speed of more than 180. With its jet-fighter profile and the spoiler mounted above its slanting tail, the Countach—one of the last of the handcrafted supercars—is arguably the fastest of all the roadsters. Since fifty-five is reachable in first gear, the coupé can top the sixty mark in 5.7 seconds, make the ton in thirteen flat.

Bolan had registered the type of bikes pursuing him. The remaining trio lined up another Gold Wing, a Harley-Davidson and a huge, 4-cyilnder, 1100cc shaft-driven BMW. None of them could touch the Lamborghini...given a straight run with no obstacles. But a five-lane city avenue crammed with lunchtime traffic is something else.

Bolan laid the Beretta in his lap as the transversely mounted five-liter V-12 behind him climbed the scale and the needles on the big twin dials flickered toward seven thousand revolutions per minute and seventy-five miles an hour in second. Through the slit rear window he could see the three bikes weaving in pursuit.

"Nice car," he said conversationally. "Hertz, Avis or Rent-a-car?"

The girl smiled briefly. "It goes with the job," she said.

Bolan leaned forward. "Okay," he said, "just for once, why not let me in on something? Surprise me. What job?"

They streaked past a line of stalled automobiles, cut between a cab and a bus pulling out from the curb, and went through a red at the Rond-Point intersection. Police whistles shrilled behind them. She flicked him a sideways glance.

"Kind of undercover," she said. "I work for the Drug Prevention Directorate of Interpol, presently allied with your Federal Narcotics Bureau."

Bolan's mouth gaped. "But I thought you were Trey-net's miss—That is to say, I figured you for..." He shrugged. "I thought you were shacked up with the guy."

"That's the disagreeable part of the job," she said. "Driving the Lambo's the other side of the coin. My brief is to get next to J.E. and uncover enough to bust his drug racket. Any way I can."

Bolan looked out the rear window again. The BMW 1100 was very close, although the rider needed both hands to thread his way through the traffic, and the Ingram had been stuffed back inside his leather Windbreaker. The other two bikes were one hundred yards farther back.

"What do you know about this Eagle's Nest scene?" Bolan asked suddenly.

Eliane shifted into third. The Lamborghini surged past Marbeuf, past la Boétie, past George V. Red brake lights on the cars ahead streamed toward the windshield like enemy tracers in a war movie. "Seems it is the nerve center of the racket," she said, twitching the wheel to avoid a student on a moped. "Even I don't know exactly where, but it's some-place near Grenoble."

"It has something to do with a village called La Trinité in the Vercors," Bolan said. He told her what he had discov-ered in the company register...was it only fifteen minutes ago?

"That poor kid," he said. "Chantal. How come you sent her to me?"

The girl shot another red light. "She wanted out. I heard them talking about you—who you were, what you did—back at the château," she said. "I don't know your angle on this deal, but I figured maybe you could help each other, is all."

"She helped me a hell of a lot more than I helped her," Bolan said sadly. He decided to confide in the blonde. It was, after all, the second time, directly or indirectly—no, shit, the third—that she had helped him out. "My angle is, well, I guess we're on the same track. Only it's the extremist political setup, this terrorist racket I want to bust wide open. Chantal told me how it works. The drug scene's an important part of it, I know. But I'm going to take apart the whole damned thing, the whole lousy stinking plot. From top to bottom.''

Eliane nodded. ''We could go on helping each other. I'd be glad to stay tuned-in and pass along any information you could use, so long as I don't risk blowing my cover, of course.''

''Yeah,'' Bolan said. ''But how did you get tuned-in in the first place? I mean, okay, you heard them talking about me at the château. Sure. But, just for starters, how come you knew where I was holed up in Paris? How did you know I'd be on the rue de Rivoli this morning? And how the hell did they know? How did they know I'd be calling by Chantal's pad last night?''

''I guess he was tailed.'' Tires shrieked as the Lamborghini shot toward the Arc de Triomphe.

Bolan said, ''You'll help out so long as you don't risk blowing your cover, right? But haven't you done that already? I mean, this buggy isn't exactly inconspicuous! Those creeps behind saw you pick me up. Won't they go straight to the boss?''

''It's a risk I took,'' she said. ''I heard about your reputation. I was kind of relying on the fact that none of them would be *around* to report back to J.E.''

Bolan grinned. ''I'll do my best, lady,'' he said.

''In the meantime that BMW is still glued to our tail, and the others are not far behind. It we get stalled at the merry-go-round beyond the arch, they could be alongside in tenths of a second. What do you want me to do?''

For the third time he squinted through the thin slit of glass behind him. A panel truck and two cabs separated them from the BMW. Down the hill, two highway patrol cops kick-started their machines and wheeled after the three killers.

"Make it to the Bois de Boulogne," Bolan said. "Take the avenue Foch and cross over into the park by the route de Suresnes. I'll look after these bums somewhere down by the lake." He picked the Beretta from his lap. "Can't you hustle this jalopy along some?"

For the first time the girl smiled. The wheels shuddered as she braked from eighty down to fifty, flicked the stick into second, and flung the low-slung roadster into the traffic behind the arch.

Bolan resisted the desire to close his eyes as vehicles flashed past right and left like the symbols on a Space Invaders display screen.

Down the long stretch length of the avenue Foch, they hit 120, then they were skating across the Porte Dauphine roundabout, over the bridge and into the Bois. The BMW had run into trouble at the previous turnaround. The rider had been lucky not to quit his mount. Now, caught up by his companions, he was three hundred yards behind, leaning almost flat into the curves in his frenzy to stay on their tail. The warble of police sirens was some way behind.

"You never answered my questions," Bolan said.

She shifted into fourth for the first time. "Which questions?"

"You didn't answer a single goddamn one."

"Try me again."

"Like how did the bastards who ordered the booby-trapping of my car get onto me within a couple of hours of my arrival in Paris? And why would they want to do that, anyway? You say your boyfriend's goons were talking about me at the château, but how did they know who I was? How come they've been ahead of me all along the line?"

"Someone recognized you in Geneva."

"Come again?"

"You were with some big shot from the administration, crafting a cover identity. Drawing money, fixing ID papers, documents and like that. This guy knew you both by sight. You don't know him. He wondered what was going on, so he tailed you. He has the means to chisel the information out of the folks who supplied you.''

"Who?''

"Guy works for the Central Foreign Bureau in Europe. Name of Philip Swanton. It seems you're on their hit list. I don't know why.''

"Bolan whistled, clutching the Lambo's grab rail as the massed trees of the Bois de Boulogne rushed toward them.

He knew why.

The CFB was an American spy agency rivaling the CIA. Its one-time boss, Lee Farnsworth, had been the KGB-run Washington mole responsible for the attack on Stony Man Farm and the death of April Rose. Bolan had proved this and then killed the traitor in front of the President himself.

None of the world's intelligence agencies likes a loner, but the field men of the CFB had less reason to love Mack Bolan than most. And they would certainly have the means to keep tabs on him. Even so...

"What I don't get—'' Bolan began, frowning. "This guy Swanton—I heard Treynet mention his name when you caught me listening in at the château. But what's his angle? Why should he pass stuff about me on to these slobs? And how come you know all about it, anyway?''

"Swanton is my liaison with the Narcotics Bureau,'' Eliane said. "He talked himself into a business deal with J.E. when we first started, when I was first assigned the mission. That's his front. He makes a big thing of sharing the Treynets' political beliefs. It might even be true at that. He's not a very likable guy. He's a director of one of their companies, anyway.''

Bolan nodded. He recalled seeing the name on the list of board members for the Schmitt-Heinkel company. "But you say...you tell me that neither you nor he, neither Interpol nor the Narcotics Bureau, are concerned with the terrorist setup? Only with the drugs?''

"That's right. Why do you ask?''

"Because somehow it doesn't stack up. I'm on the CFB hit list, okay. But I can't see why Swanton would hand me to the JETs." He shrugged. "I don't see the connection. Maybe he just figured if anyone had to knock me off, it might as well be them. Save himself the trouble and ingratiate himself with Treynet. And, of course, once they'd found that I was interested in them, that would give them their own reasons." He stared ahead through the windshield, then said, "Look, just around this curve, there's an *allée* leading down through the trees. Take it and be ready to brake hard."

Clods of earth sprayed out as the Lamborghini's fat tires scrambled around the turn into the leafy forest. The car snaked once, twice, then arrowed down toward a glint of water in the distance.

"There's a parking lot and a picnic area at the next intersection," Bolan said. "Slow down enough to let me out there, and then put on speed and take the next left-hander. Okay?"

He holstered the Beretta, unlatched the gull-wing door and held it ready for a fast push.

She bit her lip. "But what will you...? Where shall...?"

"The left-hand turn takes you down to the Auteuil racetrack," he said. "There's a big event today. Park there in Lot B, behind the paddock, and wait for me. I'll be with you in thirty minutes."

"But..."

"No 'buts.' This is it."

Bolan took a swift backward glance. The bikes were not yet in sight. They hurtled across the intersection, and the roadster shuddered again as Eliane heel-and-toed, hitting the brakes and shifting down in the same movement.

Bolan pushed the door halfway up and dove out of the car, shoulder-rolling as the turf sped up to meet him. The girl leaned across to pull down the door and accelerated away.

By the time the bikes appeared, Bolan was prone at the foot of a grassy bank beside the trail. This part of the Bois was deserted. The first race at Auteuil was due anytime. He could hear the murmur of the crowd over the sighing of wind in the treetops. Even the whores who usually patrolled the woods were placing their bets. Or maybe having lunch, Bolan thought. In France everything stops for lunch.

Except perhaps murder. The roar of the bikes drowned out the race crowd. Bolan wormed his way to the top of the bank, the big stainless-steel AutoMag between his hands.

The Lambo was vanishing around a bend farther down the ride. The bikers were catching up fast now, flattened along their tanks, but they wouldn't have seen the Executioner leave the car.

Bolan took his weight on his elbows, tracking the gun as the machines drew level. He fired three shots at the BMW, still slightly in the lead.

The first was wide, just ahead of the front wheel. The second slammed into the alloy disk between the hub and the rim. The third took the rider in the thigh.

But before that the impact of the heavy slug on the front wheel had knocked the steering through ninety degrees, wrenching the handlebars from the biker's grasp. The BMW, traveling at something over ninety miles an hour, nose-dived.

The killer was already on his way out of the saddle when he was hit. He arched through the air for thirty feet, landing on his back with a thump that left him stunned. The bike somersaulted, engine howling, then crashed to the ground and stalled.

Past the spinning rear wheel Bolan was already lining up on the second machine, the Harley-Davidson, which imposed a more upright seat on the rider. The guy was braking hard. He was trying to avoid the BMW and simultaneously work out what the hell had happened to it.

He never knew. Bolan's three-group punched him in the chest, punctured leather, T-shirt, flesh, bone and lung tissue before making a single exit wound so wide that the trees were visible beyond it.

Bike and rider toppled over, littering the turf with blood and guts as the machine whizzed around like a crazy catherine wheel or an aerosoled fly.

Bringing up the rear, the man on the Honda was smart. While Bolan was downing the other two, he had time to react...and to think.

He braked some and then wheeled the bike around in a foot-assisted slide, thrust it to the side of the trail and rode down the slope and in among the trees.

Bolan cursed. Zapping the enemy one at a time always made problems. But if he had waited, allowed them to line up one on either side and one in front, he would have been the deadest duck out of the air.

He leaped to his feet and ran for a thick belt of undergrowth, hearing the highway patrolmen's sirens advance in the distance. The biker was armed with an Ingram MAC-11, and two handguns were not going to best that in the open, even if they did share almost the same caliber ammunition.

The shrill stammer of the machine pistol desecrated the noonday quiet as Bolan made it beneath the bushes on elbows and knees. He exhausted the remainder of Big Thunder's magazine in the general direction of the biker's hideout—a thicket fifty yards away—and then slammed in a flesh clip, readying the Beretta in his other hand.

The killer fired again, a long burst that zipped through the foliage just above Bolan's head. A six-inch-thick oak sapling, almost cut in two by the spray, leaned over, split with a splintering sound and crashed to the ground. Now the guy would have to reload, Bolan figured. He loosed a couple of 3-shot blasts, one from each gun—if the enemy thought there were two of them, so much the better—and dashed for a fern-covered depression farther into the forest.

Once in this new location he restricted himself to the silenced Beretta, firing two short bursts. If the gunman couldn't tell where the shots originated, he might reveal himself in trying to get a better view.

He did. A sinister helmeted figure edged around the inside of the thicket, his back to the young stems, the muzzle of the Ingram questing left and right.

Bolan was six feet up in the lowest fork of a birch tree, above the depression. He emptied the Beretta's magazine.

Crash helmets are designed to withstand the impact of a fifty-pound weight dropped from a certain height, but not the assault of subsonic 9mm boattails traveling at muzzle velocities of nearly eleven hundred feet per second. Bolan saw that the visor was sprayed red. Blood streamed down inside the chin guard to soak the gunman's neck and shoulders. He fell forward onto the Ingram.

Simultaneously Bolan felt a searing pain, a red-hot iron laid across his left arm, and registered only later the rip-roar chatter of another MAC-11 from the trail. Leaves from the savaged branches above fluttered past his face.

The rider of the BMW had overcome the slug in his thigh sufficiently to crawl behind his werecked bike and line up his sights on the Executioner in his tree.

Bolan dropped to the ground, took Big Thunder and let it rip.

The BMW's tank ruptured, another slug struck metal and produced sparks, the high-octane fuel ignited. Instantly the guy was a flaming fireball, thrashing helplessly on the ground.

The sirens were very near now, groaning down the scale as the patrolmen slowed. Let them work out the connection between three dead punks in the Bois de Boulogne and another responsible for the mayhem on the rue de Rivoli.

Bolan vanished among the trees.

By the lake he tore off the sleeve of his shirt and washed the wound in his left arm. It was no more than a crease, a raw furrow through the flesh of his forearm. It would be stiff for a couple of days, but neither bone nor muscle were damaged. He bound it up as best he could with the sleeve and headed for the track.

The Lamborghini was in Parking Lot B, all right.

But of Eliane Falcoz, although he waited around until the end of the big race, there was no sign.

He took a cab back to the city center, checked out of his hotel and headed for the airport at Orly.

The Executioner had business to attend to in Grenoble.

11

"You were lucky we had that last-minute cancellation," the pretty redhead behind the reception desk told Mack Bolan when he checked into the Hôtel Majestic at Grenoble. "Every hotel in town has been taken on account of the congress."

"Congress?"

She stared at him. "You didn't even know? But I thought that was why you—It's right here in this hotel. The eliminating round of the World Masters' Tournament. You know," she explained kindly, "chess."

"Oh," Bolan said. "Yeah? Well I guess I better go on up and stash this gear in my room just the same." He took his key, smiled, picked up his lightweight holdall and headed for the elevator bank.

The Majestic was a large nineteenth-century hotel built around a huge central rotunda in the days when space was affordable. There was a circular gallery beneath the dome, and below this an open space customarily dotted with leather easy chairs, occasional tables and palms in wooden tubs. The management referred to it either as the Rotunda Lounge or the Palm Court, depending on whether a piano and fiddle duo happened to be playing on the small stage opposite the entrance.

For the chess congress, the black-and-white marble floor had been cleared and several tiers of spectator seats installed around a central area where the games took place beneath numerous high arches.

With his incisive, evaluative mind, Bolan would have made a fine player, but in fact he had little interest in chess. The game to which he was devoted made use of human pieces on a board that was worldwide, a game where bishops and royalty made only minor appearances, where there were always castles to be stormed, but no gallant knights and far too many pawns sacrificed.

Nevertheless, leaving his room sometime later, Bolan paused on his way down to the reception area and glanced over the rail of the gallery at the scene below.

Complete quiet in the huge lounge. The spectators leaned forward in their seats, collectively holding their breaths. Above and behind the fringe of potted plants at the edge of the stage a television crew silently manipulated a camera. Beneath the blazing lights four games were in progress.

The names of the competitors—Korchnoi, Karpov, Ludovic, Watson—were slotted into metal frames above each table. Idly, Bolan regarded the game immediately below him, which, according to the nameplates, was between a Yugoslav, Anton Sujic, and a Soviet, Mikhail Orlov.

There were few pieces left on the board. After a period of intense concentration, the Russian moved his queen diagonally to the far right-hand side of the board and murmured, "Check!"

He punched the clock fixed to the side of the table, pushed back his chair and stood. Sujic fingered a small goatee and studied the board.

Orlov was a sturdy man with a bushy mustache and iron-gray hair cut short in the eastern European manner. He moved away from the table carrying a plate on which were balanced a glass of Russian tea and several slices of lemon. He drank the tea.

Sujic suddenly moved his knight, punched the clock and sat back with a smile.

The Russian returned to the table and set down his empty glass. He studied the board, his brow furrowed in concentration. Absently, he picked up one of the lemon slices and began to chew it.

Bolan froze.

Orlov swallowed, placed another slice in his mouth.

By the time he moved, twelve minutes later, all the lemon slices were gone.

Bolan grasped the rail of the gallery, expelling his breath slowly. There was not a shadow of a doubt. The disguise was perfect but that one little idiosyncrasy had given him away.

Only one man in the world that Bolan knew of chewed up and then swallowed the lemon segments when he drank tea.

Strakhov.

Bolan's mortal enemy, Major General Greb Strakhov, boss of the KGB's Thirteenth Section—the sector of the First Chief Directorate responsible for Executive Action. In short, an international murder squad.

Strakhov, whose planners had run the mole Lee Farnsworth and were thus responsible for the death of April Rose.

Strakhov, who had masterminded the Stony Man debacle in revenge for the death of his only son, killed by Bolan during a secret mission in Russia.

Strakhov, whose seven hundred thousand agents throughout the world had been given a detailed description of Mack Bolan...and instructions to kill him on sight.

What the hell was he doing here?

That the Russian was a chess buff, an ex-Grand Master in fact, Bolan knew; the game was reputed to be the KGB chief's only diversion. It also kept his mind sharpened, in tune with the forward planning and analysis of an opponent's probable moves inseparable from his undercover work.

But to find him, in disguise, apparently therefore using chess merely as a cover, so near to the Treynet headquarters—surely that was no coincidence?

Was Strakhov for once effectively running in harness with Bolan, seeking to eradicate the neo-Fascist danger represented by the Treynets and their slaves?

Bolan did not think so.

But he had to find out for sure. With an enemy as powerful as Strakhov, it was vital to know whether or not they were by chance playing in the same game.

At the newsstand in the reception hall he bought a large-scale map of the Vercors region. La Trinité-en-Royans was no more than fifteen miles from the city as the crow flies. But the minor roads that led there were anything but straight, and the country was hilly. Bolan figured it would be about an hour's drive.

As he folded the map, a crowd of spectators left the congress hall. "I don't get the Ruskies," one of them complained. "This guy Orlov had the Yugoslav over a barrel— three moves max, and it would have been checkmate—and then suddenly he concedes. He throws in the towel and gives the game to Sujic! What do you make of that?"

Bolan didn't wait to hear the reply. He knew what to make of it. He was already on his way to the reception area.

Strakhov was a man who hated to lose. If he was handing a game to an opponent when he was in a winning position it could only mean one thing: the game was no more than a blind, as Bolan had surmised. Strakhov had more important things to do, things that clearly had to be done by a certain time.

Bolan decided to tag along.

At the desk, he said, "Sorry. I forgot to sign the register when I checked in. If you'd lend me a pen...?"

The redhead smiled and spun the heavy book. Bolan signed, glanced over the previous entries. "Orlov" had signed in the previous day. What was more interesting was the name immediately below his.

Dr. D. Schmitt-Heinkel from Frankfurt.

One of them was in 821, the other in 823. If the hotel rooms were numbered the usual way, that meant they were in adjoining suites; 822 would be on the opposite side of the corridor.

Interesting.

Bolan headed for the elevators.

He was in 735. Strakhov and the guy who lent his name to Treynet's drug manufactory should be on the floor above, nearer the gallery.

Bolan was on the fire escape, wearing his blacksuit, crouched down outside 821 when the Russian spy master came upstairs. Venetian blinds masked the windows but there was a crack between two slats through which the Executioner could survey most of the room.

Strakhov's behavior when he entered the room was unexpected. He locked the outer door carefully, then produced a key from a chain looped across his vest and unlocked the connecting door between his suite and the next. He walked into Dr. Schmitt-Heinkel's room and closed the door.

Bolan didn't get it. Okay, it was a link between Strakhov and the Treynet camp. But what the hell could it mean?

He couldn't see inside 823 from the fire escape. By the time the door to the corridor opened, he was in a broom cupboard halfway to the elevators, peeking through the smallest crack.

Two men came out of 823.

Bolan caught his breath. The first was Lange, the German gorilla so anxious to lay hands on him at the vacation camp. The second was clearly Dr. Schmitt-Heinkel—a fat, clean-shaven, jowly man with curling white hair, thick tortoise-shell glasses and a loud check suit.

He was also Major General Greb Strakhov.

It was not too difficult when you were alerted and expecting something tricky. But the link was not only there, it was a damn sight closer than Bolan had imagined.

Orlov, Strakhov and Schmitt-Heinkel were one and the same person.

THE RENTED CITROËN that the red-haired receptionist had obtained for Bolan at short notice from "a friend in the business" was no match for the Opel Capitan speeding Strakhov and Lange along the die-straight highway that led south into the mountains from Grenoble. But once the Opel turned onto the network of minor roads webbing the lower slopes of the Vercors, the smaller car had no difficulty keeping up.

Bolan stayed a discreet distance behind. Within a half hour of leaving the hotel it became clear that the KGB chief was indeed, as Bolan had assumed, on his way to La Trinité.

The night before, he had been forced to let them go. He had no transport, and he could scarcely escape attention promenading the streets of the city in nothing but a skin-tight blacksuit.

Today, having checked that "Orlov" had no game scheduled until late afternoon, he had been ready for them when they left.

Strakhov was in his Schmitt-Heinkel role once more. Bolan was intrigued. Did Lange, the Fascist strong-arm, accept his companion at face value—as a German right-winger who for some reason chose to pass himself off as a Russian chess player? Or was he wise to the spy master's real identity? In other words, was he a dupe or in the pay of the KGB?

Bolan hoped eventually to move in close enough to overhear their conversation. That should give him a clue to their relationship.

In the meantime he was alert to take in anything and everything that could help advance the mission. Right now that meant, in addition to shadowing the Opel, a detailed recon of the terrain.

It was a sunny morning. As the green slopes of the Isère Valley dropped away from the frowning limestone heights closed in on either side, he was increasingly aware how smart the Treynets had been in choosing this wild area as a headquarters.

There are very few roads climbing to the plateau that tops the Vercors massif, and each one is visible along its entire length from the rocky escarpment bordering the region. The plateau consists of upland prairie alternating with forest country, much of it more than five thousand feet above sea level. It is a desolate landscape of isolated villages and small farms.

Easy enough, therefore, to post lookouts and keep a check on who might be heading your way.

The big Opel climbed past Claix, past Villard, and then through a pass breaching a ridge sheltering Pont-en-Royans. La Trinité lay in the triangle between this village, Saint-Jean-en-Royans and the seven-thousand-foot summit of Mount Aiguille.

It was a dead village. More than half the somber gray houses on its single street were abandoned, and many of the others had boarded-up windows.

Smart of the Treynets again—no neighbors to gossip.

The Opel continued for another mile and then swung right onto a side road marked as a cul-de-sac. Grass grew in the center of the narrow track, but there was a freshly painted notice board beside the road sign.

PRIVATE PROPERTY—NO ENTRY!
SCHMITT-HEINKEL SA
EAGLE CHEMICALS
No admittance without official pass

He continued along the main road, which was sign-posted to Die and Valence. It would be asking for trouble to follow the Opel along an empty driveway with no exit, most of it probably under observation anyway. The last thing he wanted was to tip off Strakhov that he was being followed.

A quarter of a mile along the road he stopped the Citroën beneath a row of poplars and climbed a bank with Konzaki's field glasses. Across the rolling upland he saw the

Opel, beetle-bright in the sunshine, moving along the trail beside a field of ripening corn. Beyond the field was a wood, and rising above that a limestone cliff about 150 feet high.

Bolan swept the binoculars right and left. The trail ran right up to the cliff and—it was difficult to see because young trees grew between the rocks there—but, yeah, a cleft divided two great masses of limestone, and the road ran right into a natural defile splitting the face of the escarpment.

He adjusted the focus. The cleft was in deep shadow but the red Triphium light source brightened the gloom, threw the image into sharper relief.

Bolan could see that the crevasse ran only a short way before it was blocked by a wall of rock.

Through this inner face a tunnel had been blasted.

At the mouth of the tunnel two heavies, armed and uniformed like the hardmen outside the vacation camp, stood between a gatekeeper's hut and a barrier pole. On the cliff top far above, two other men stood guard.

The Opel paused by the shack. The pole rose. The car moved forward and was swallowed up in the blackness of the tunnel.

The Strakhov-Treynet link was complete.

EXCEPT THAT THE ROCK was limestone, pale silver-gray in the spring sunshine, the place could have been a mesa in New Mexico, with the difference that the top, instead of being flat, was dished—a saucer-shaped depression maybe a mile and a half across and two to three hundred feet deep at the center. Other than scaling the vertical cliffs on the outside, the only way in to this landscape bowl was through the tunnel Bolan had seen.

"Nobody knows who made the tunnels," the helicopter pilot told him. "But several of the roads leading up to the Vercors pass through the rock."

"Maybe they enlarged existing passages," Bolan said. "The region's famous for its caves and grottoes, isn't it?"

"Honeycombed," the pilot said.

"Is that one of the older tunnels?" Bolan pointed down through the Plexiglas to the cleft where he had seen the Opel disappear.

"Search me." The pilot shrugged. "You could tell, looking at it. The new ones, the ones got enlarged, you can see the marks where they drilled the rock to lay the charges."

"I got the idea they don't particularly welcome visitors down there," Bolan said.

"I wouldn't know," said the pilot. "Some kind of a factory, I think. German. They tell me there's a research center there, too." He laughed. "Maybe they're scared the rubbernecks would steal the secret formula for the latest brand of aspirin."

"Maybe," Bolan said.

He scanned the terrain once more. It was clear, even from three thousand feet, that this was the stronghold he had so far failed to locate. The place was a natural fortress.

The steep slopes were patrolled by men handling dogs in pairs. The shotguns slung across their backs glinted in the sun. Bolan could see wire fencing. He did not need to be told that this was probably electrified and that the cliff faces would be crisscrossed with trip wires and planted with electronic sensors.

The factory was a single-story building with multiple serrated roofs slanted to snare the southern light. Behind it, panel trucks were backed up to loading bays in a row of prefab storehouses.

No prizes, Bolan reflected grimly, for guessing what products were refined beneath those roofs and then packaged and distributed at rock-bottom prices from the sheds behind: opium, cocaine, heroin, morphine, amphetamines, purple hearts, poppers—anything for kicks.

Join the JETs set and show the oldsters what youth can do! Yeah, and chuck decency, respect for the lives of others and every single goddamn rule you ever learned out the window. Mail a letter bomb today! Fire a gun for freedom, and the hell with who gets hurt! Live now, baby, and vote later.

Or else.

Hell, there were some slimeballs the world could do without, creeps who could dream up a routine like that. Well, the Executioner would do his damnedest to help the world get what it wanted.

The pilot was looking at him curiously. "You want to fly over to the Rhône Valley and check it out from that side?" he asked.

"Sure," Bolan said.

He had hired the chopper from a private charter company based on the airfield at Grenoble. It was an old Bell AH-1G Huey Cobra that had somehow found its way to Europe via the Vietnam black market, mercenaries in Africa and the Middle East arms bazaar. Bolan's story was that he wanted to check out locations for a big-budget war movie, to see how well the terrain lent itself to aerial shots of battle.

And it was going to be a battle all right, getting inside that place solo and doing what he had to do. And the air recon was vital.

The charter people had not thought the request anything out of the ordinary. Most of their clients wanted to overfly tracts of country for some special screwball reason: prospecting for vacation sites, photographing property for sale, surveying the area for developers.

Bolan didn't want to attract attention by circling over the Eagle's Nest; he had not told the pilot he was especially interested in that part of the Vercors. He reckoned that two passes, one flying west, the other returning, should not raise suspicions below. There were always helicopters around: fire-prevention crews, police patrols, training flights, mountain-rescue teams.

On the way back he looked more closely at a building behind the factory. It was an old rambling house with two wings and pantiled roofs at a dozen different levels. Probably the original farmhouse when the enclosed valley had been an agricultural estate.

Now it was surrounded by formal gardens, an Olympic-size pool and a graveled turnaround on which a dozen cars were parked.

Bolan craned forward in the front of the Huey Cobra's two tandem seats. Using the binoculars he could make out a Rolls-Royce, Schmitt-Heinkel's Opel, several large American sedans and a scarab-green Lamborghini Countach.

Beyond the gardens, wooden chalets were ranged around an open space in a way that reminded him of an army camp and parade ground.

"You know something?" The pilot leaned forward and spoke over Bolan's shoulder to make himself heard above the Lycoming turboshaft. "In your epoch, I mean the epoch of the story you're shooting, in 1944, there were thirty-five hundred guys in the marquis holed up down there on the Vercors. They held off two armored divisions of Krauts—tanks and flamethrowers and artillery and all—for more than two months. Proclaimed an independent state of Free France slap in the middle of the fuckin' occupation! They say you could see the French tricolor flying above the church in Vassieux clear down to the city."

"No kidding," Bolan said. He was memorizing every detail of the property, the relation of roads, buildings and open spaces to trees and scrub below. His life could depend on this memory.

"'Course, when the SS finally blasted in there," the pilot said, "they gave the survivors hell. Tortured the guys before they hanged them. Raped the women. Cut off their tits with shears and stuffed pick handles up their—"

"Yeah," Bolan said. "I heard."

Some of those brave patriots, he guessed, probably made their last stand in the depression below, waiting for the allied airlift with arms and reinforcements that never came.

What a bitter irony that forty years later the place should become the bastion and retreat of a new fascism, its emblem no longer the French flag but a reborn Nazi eagle....

DR. DIETER SCHMITT-HEINKEL, AKA Mikhail Orlov, AKA Major General Greb Strakhov of the KGB, stared angrily at the man who called himself Lange. They had just parked the Opel in the multistory lot beside the Majestic.

"Are you telling me, Alexei Simeonovitch, that your men have still not regained contact with the criminal Bolan?" he demanded.

Lange shifted his feet. When the major general used the patronymic form of address it meant trouble. The shadow of the gulag, at best of manual labor in the smelting works of Magnitogorsk, hung over every operation that was considered unsatisfactory when you worked for the Thirteenth Section. He swallowed.

"It was known that he went to the register of companies, Comrade General," he said awkwardly. "It was Treynet's young fools who fouled up after that. We never thought he would get away. By the time it was realized that he had killed all four of them he had already checked out of his hotel. It was not the fault of the men from the embassy."

"I am not interested in faults," Strakhov said icily. "I am interested in results."

"Yes, Comrade General. Of course. I am sorry. We did what we—"

"Where is he now?"

"Here. Somewhere here in the city. We assume he had found out about the Eagle's Nest from the company register. We were told at the hotel that he was booked on the flight to Grenoble yesterday afternoon."

"But nobody was bright enough to pick him up here? Knowing how sensitive the operation is at this time, how near to the crucial phase we are, knowing that this capitalist lickspittle is interesting himself in our affairs, knowing he was on his way... Nobody picked him up when he arrived?"

"No, sir," Lange said wretchedly. "You see, by the time we discovered he was booked on that flight, the plane had already landed."

"Brilliant," growled Strakhov. "You have allowed him to get away three times, Alexei Simeonovitch. Unless you have a particular liking for the country to the east of the Urals, I would recommend that you avoid a fourth." A vein in his temple suddenly throbbed. His face flushed red. "The criminal Bolan must be located and exterminated," he shouted. "Do I make myself clear?"

"Yes, Comrade General," Lange said.

CROUCHED BEHIND THE RENTED CITROËN in the adjacent parking slot, Bolan allowed his breath to escape as the two men moved away.

The picture was becoming clearer. Lange was no dupe. With his obsequious "Yes, Comrade General; no, Comrade General," it was evident that he was in the KGB plot up to his neck.

He must be some kind of mole working for Strakhov inside the Treynets' extreme right-wing setup.

Why?

Not for the good of democracy, that was for sure.

Strakhov himself must therefore be a supermole. It was too much to expect that either of the Treynets knew that their partner in the drug business was a communist agent!

Bolan hurried to the main post office, exchanged a couple of hundred-franc bills for a handful of coins, and shut himself inside a phone booth. It was early afternoon in eastern France, commuters' morning rush hour stateside. If he was lucky he might catch Hal Brognola at home.

He fed coins into the box, direct dialed a number in the United States.

When the phone had rung four times he replaced the handset and dialed again. This time he hung up after three rings. Next time he dialed the line was opened at once, although nobody answered.

Bolan enunciated a code phrase identifying himself.

When his voiceprint had been accepted by the sophisticated electronic hookup at the other end, an emotionless computerized voice pronounced a number, repeated it twice, and then the line went dead.

Memorizing the number—it changed twice each day—Bolan dropped in more money and dialed it out.

A girl's voice said, "Yes, please?"

Bolan gave her a second code identifier and asked to be connected to Brognola, wherever he was. The presidential liaison was on the line in less than a minute.

Bolan spoke rapidly, guardedly, since it was an open line, and posed one question.

The reply was phoned through to his hotel room before dark that evening.

It was in effect a complete rundown on the person, principles and practices of a certain Dr. Dieter Schmitt-Heinkel, resident severally in Frankfurt and Munich, president of a small but increasingly vociferous neo-Fascist political party in Bavaria.

The Herr Doktor, according to the dossier, was often away from home. That figured. He had to take time out to be Strakhov, and Strakhov also had other fish to fry, other irons in the fire, other plots to hatch. The KGB's subversion program had always been as diverse as the metaphors used to describe it.

The Herr Doktor visited France often and was thought to be seeking political allies in that country.

It was known that he had been the driving force behind the formation, three years ago, of the right-wing Franco-Teuton Bund, whose chairman was a certain Jacques Edouard Treynet.

The Herr Doktor had first come to prominence—and thus into the data banks of the world's intelligence services—with the formation of his south German minority party in 1979.

Comrade Strakhov had been burrowing his molelike way into the neo-Fascist ranks for more than five years.

A plot as deeply laid, involving so much planning, must therefore be of paramount importance to the KGB.

What ulterior motive could justify to the politburo, the Soviet Council of Ministers and the guys who held the purse strings, such as extravagant outlay of time, men and money?

How could such a fabricated alliance benefit world communism?

Bolan knew enough of Soviet thinking, and of KGB methods in particular, to hazard an informed guess.

Strakhov, his associates and their organizations—formed specially for the purpose—were swinging all their weight behind the Treynets in furtherance of their diabolical scheme. They were pushing the drug conspiracy, encouraging the terrorism, egging on the French right-wingers in every way until the day they made their play.

But there would be a double bluff involved.

Once the neo-Fascists had succeeded in creating a climate of terror, a totally anarchic situation, and had used their bludgeoned voters to strong-arm their way to power...then it would be the Communists' turn.

Strakhov and his accomplices would renege on their duped partners.

Oh, not openly. Hell, no. "Schmitt-Heinkel," "Lange" and the others would simply retire, but their inside knowledge would be used to expose the entire Treynet villainy from start to finish for the world to see.

Just the way Mack Bolan himself wanted to do it.

Except that the aim would not be quite the same.

Having blown the Treynet plot apart, the forces of communism, still masterminded by Strakhov's KGB, would step in and seize power themselves—with the explanation and the excuse that would justify the putsch in the eyes of the world—look, we saved you from another Hitler.

12

"Outrage in Lyons!" the two-inch newspaper headline screamed. A parcel bomb had exploded in the baggage check at Lyons-Perrache railroad station during the rush hour. Twelve killed and sixty-eight injured.

On an inside page, a news item reported that a judge and a district attorney had been gunned down outside a courthouse near Marseilles. Ex-convicts with a grudge were thought responsible for the murders.

Teenage gangsters had killed a cashier, a store detective and three shoppers with a burp gun during a supermarket holdup in the north. They had gotten away with nearly six thousand in cash.

A leading article syndicated in the newspaper chain owned by Jules Treynet reminded readers of the unexplained deaths in the Bois de Boulogne and the massacre on the rue de Rivoli, calling for stronger measures to deal with the wave of violence.

At the newsstand in the Hôtel Majestic in Grenoble, Alexei Simeonovitch Lange, whose real family name was Golopkin, scanned a newspaper and smiled. The operation was progressing according to plan.

It was purely by chance that he looked up and saw Bolan.

The Executioner had, in fact, checked out of the hotel very early. If Strakhov and his minions knew he was in town, it would be crazy to stick around when he could be recognized at any time. He would find a new base outside the city. Meanwhile he had things to do. But first he must

wait until the red-haired receptionist came on duty so that
he could arrange to rent the Citroën a few days more.

Seeing the big guy bending over the desk, Lange drew
back quickly behind a potted plant. Strakhov, as Orlov,
would be occupied in the congress hall all morning. Here
was a chance for Lange to show that the servant could be as
smart as the master, smarter if he liquidated the damned
American, for Strakhov had repeatedly tried to do just that.

Behind a postcard stand, Lange overheard Bolan telling
the girl goodbye. He would be collecting the Citroën from
the parking lot and leaving Grenoble for a couple of days.

Lange raised his paper. Holding it over one side of his
face, he sidled past a glassed-in phone booth. A dark man
with a heavy mustache seemed to be having trouble making
a connection with a number in Morocco. Lange walked
through the revolving doors to the sidewalk. The Opel was
parked at the curb.

Three minutes later, Lange turned the car into the narrow lane that ran between the hotel and the multistory
parking lot. Bolan was halfway along beneath the window-
less side of the building, striding toward the side entrance
reserved for pedestrians. The other side of the lane was
bounded by an eight-foot brick wall enclosing the yard
where the Majestic kitchen personnel put out their trash
cans, received deliveries and hung laundry to dry.

Lange allowed the Opel to glide in second to within
twenty yards of the Executioner. Then, judging his time
nicely, he stamped the gas pedal flat. The big sedan leaped
forward, laying rubber on the cobbled lane.

The passage boasted no sidewalk; it was no more than
three yards wide. Trapped between two solid walls, Bolan
had no place to go.

Yet something, some sixth sense, some battle-tested re-
flex tipped him off to danger in the instant that Lange
stamped the throttle. Before the Opel was under way he was
on the move, hurling himself to the far side of the lane.

Lange grinned. The gate leading to the hotel yard was fifty feet away.

He tweaked the wheel. The Opel's steel bumper and grill arrowed toward the target.

Then, at the very last instant, Bolan jumped upward. His fingers closed over the ledge on top of the wall and he swung his legs forward and up as the sedan thundered toward him.

It was an acrobatic feat that could only have been achieved by a man in peak condition whose muscles were supertuned.

Mack Bolan was such a man.

He hooked the heel of one foot over the ledge and was able to exert enough leverage to heave his body out of danger as the Opel was on him.

Sparks flew as the fender scraped the wall beneath his jackknifed body.

Lange swore, steered the car away from the brickwork. There was a clatter as a strip of chrome was ripped from the Opel and fell to the ground.

It was useless trying again, once the element of surprise had been lost. And he dared not back up and use a gun. Bolan was on top of the wall and he was probably armed. In any case, Lange dared not risk any scandal that would compromise his status, and therefore that of Strakhov, as a peaceful German citizen with an industrial interest in the region and a partnership with a prominent Frenchman based in the Vercors. It would be difficult enough already, explaining to the KGB chief how the Opel had gotten damaged.

Lange drove through the lane.

In the rearview he saw Bolan jump lightly to the ground and trot unhurriedly toward the lot. The image was too small for him to be 100 percent certain, but Lange could have sworn the big guy was grinning. He gritted his teeth, feeling a pulse at the side of his jaw swell and begin to pound.

In a residential square two blocks away, he parked the Opel and settled down to wait. The roads behind the hotel, all one-way, were arranged in such a way that Bolan would have to pass through the square.

In the meantime there was work to be done. Lange unhooked a UHF radio mike from beneath the dash. He contacted the man in charge of the half-dozen operatives, ostensibly clerks and chauffeurs but in reality KGB field agents, who had been sent from the Soviet Embassy in Paris to help him. They were in a rented house on the northwestern outskirts of the city.

"Basically, there are only three ways he can go," Lange told the guy. "West to Lyons, north to Chambéry and Switzerland, or back south into the mountains. I'll stick to him when he shows and fill you in on his route. Then you can take over, but you'll have to move fast. He must be ambushed and disposed of before he gets to wherever he's going. That is imperative."

He listened to the voice quacking in the scuttle-mounted receiver, then said, "Yes. Very well. We shall plan it as we go along. Once we have seen which direction the criminal takes, an opportunity will present itself. The important thing is to be ready at all times.... If you think we may need help, I will call in operatives from our trade delegation in Geneva."

Lange broke off the conversation with a hurried "Be in touch," and replaced the mike. He slid behind the wheel and twisted the key in the ignition. Bolan's old Citroën was entering the square.

Lange gave him a couple of hundred yards and then nosed the Opel out after him.

The American took a broad avenue that followed the course of the Isère River, turned left over a bridge, and joined a stream of weekend traffic climbing the access strip to the A41 turnpike.

So it was to be Chambéry after all. Wondering why Bolan would be heading in that direction, Lange called his accomplices and briefed them on his position. From where they were waiting in three separate cars, they should be able to make it to the next access strip and drive onto the turnpike ahead of the Citroën. They could then hang in until Bolan passed them, taking over the chase from Lange.

He gave them the license number of Bolan's car.

Lange made no attempt to conceal the fact that he was tailing the Citroën. With its offside fender buckled and one headlamp smashed, the Opel was no easy car to hide, anyway.

If the American was aware—as he would be, since Lange had tried to run him down—that he was being shadowed, he would be concentrating on the Opel, less likely to get wise to the other tails.

If he did catch on, there was a chance he would quit the turnpike and try to wriggle his way out of the trap among the minor roads.

Lange's rocklike face fissured into an anticipatory smile. That would be just fine. If they caught up with the bastard in a country area where there were no witnesses, they could use the RPG-7 grenade launcher that would be in one of the embassy cars.

The A41 runs for thirty miles along the lower valley of the Isère, shadowed on the right by the Belledonne Alpine Foothills and on the left by the steep limestone escarpment known as the Grande Chartreuse.

Lange saw the three KGB-manned cars—a Renault 30, Skoda coupé and Russian Lada, all locally licensed—when they were five miles from the city. They were not bunched together; two were in the slow lane, separated by a huge semi with Swiss plates, and the Skoda coupé was in the center lane some distance ahead.

Bolan's Citroën steamed past them in the outside lane, comfortably above the legal seventy-five miles an hour limit. Lange dropped back. It was not all that easy, laying a box on a single car that morning.

The road was the equivalent of an American interstate, and it was crowded. Although it was a gray day threatening rain, the Grenoblois weekenders raced three abreast toward their country chalets, the boating at Aiguebelette, the pony-trek schools, a hang-glider station near Saint-Pierre-de-Chartreuse.

Go too fast and you get carried past your quarry in a covey of boy-racers. Lag behind and you're a rock in a stream, the current dividing to flow around you, changing lanes and fraying tempers right and left. Brake hard and you risk setting up a shock wave that would screech rubber and crumple fenders all the way back to the city.

Bolan passed the exits for Domène, Saint Pierre and Goncelin. The flow slackened. As sometimes happens on a limited-speed highway when the traffic makes its own rules, there was a bunch of vehicles and then a sudden gap. Lange saw three empty lanes for half a mile ahead. For the moment there was nothing coming up behind.

He picked up the mike.

The Renault accelerated and passed Bolan, cutting sharply into his lane. The Skoda drew level on the inside and the Russian car came abreast in the left lane.

Riding shotgun, Lange nodded his satisfaction. They would make it now, before the next wave of traffic roared near.

He spoke into the mike again. A light rain began to fall.

Bolan's play took everyone by surprise.

The Citroën made a sudden spurt, distancing the sluggish Lada, and when it was some way ahead, almost nudging the Renault, braked violently.

Seeing the lights blaze red, Lange swore. What in hell was the idiot American playing at? Making a break for the right lane? There was no exit strip for miles.

Not on their side of the turnpike there wasn't.... But on the south side a service road led to a sandy wilderness littered with heavy construction machinery, where an interchange loop was being carved into the landscape.

The Citroën swung hard left onto the median strip, cutting in front of the Lada. It swerved between two lengths of armco barriers, plowed down a row of oleanders and raced across the three lanes on the far side under the noses of two advancing trucks.

The driver of the Lada was able to follow at least as far as the oleanders. There he had to wait amid an angry blare of horns until there was a gap. Sweating, Lange plunged after the Russian sedan.

The Skoda braked, careering into a U-turn. The Renault was too far ahead to stop in time. Its driver braked and began backing up.

It was then that the two young men in the black Ferrari roared up behind them.

The Ferrari, a 308-GT4, was hitting something like 130 miles an hour.

Faced suddenly with the reversing lights of a Renault backing toward him, a Skoda athwart the center lane, and the tail end of an Opel bumping over the median strip, the young driver hesitated and then panicked. He pumped his foot frantically upon the brake.

Too late and too hard.

The fat low-pressure Pirellis lost traction on the wet pavement. The wheels locked as the driver tweaked the steering. The Ferrari slid sideways, skating toward the gap between the Opel and the Skoda, then spun around as the youth overcorrected.

The tail swung in a wide arch across the road, swiped the front end of the coupé in midturn and knocked it spinning onto its roof, then hurtled toward the Renault at top speed.

The cars collided with a jarring crash, locked together and slid across the hard shoulder and down an embankment beyond.

There was a muffled whoosh, a sudden gush of flame, and then a cloud of carmine-tinged black smoke bellying skyward.

All that Lange saw of the accident was a blur of movement in his rearview mirror. At first he did not realize that two of his cars, the Skoda and the Renault, had been put out of action. He was too busy waiting for a gap in the southbound traffic to follow the Lada across the highway.

Bolan was halfway up the slope leading to the roadworks site.

Since it was a weekend, the site was deserted. Weaving among bulldozers, dump trucks and giant earth-moving trucks, the Citroën raced to the far end of the sandy lot, where the construction crew had begun building the access strip to the highway that would eventually bridge the turnpike.

The strip had been graded and curved, although it had yet to be surfaced.

Halfway up, a second truck curled away to a wide, flat space gouged from the hillside, destined to become a rest area and gas station.

Lange was yelling into his mike as the Opel reached the site. The two cars ahead of it were clouds of yellow dust among the silent machines.

The KGB men opened fire when the Citroën was still eighty yards short of the unfinished access strip. Lange could not see the results—the rain was not yet falling heavily enough to settle the dust—but he heard the rip-roar of a submachine gun and the sharper crack of Kalashnikovs clattering against the underside of the Citroën.

He gunned the engine of the Opel. The wheels spun. The big sedan scrambled for a grip on the rough ground and then lurched forward.

Abruptly the dust cleared. On stony ground now, Lange saw that the Lada had stopped. The three men crewing the car had spread out, two of them behind an enormous red-striped concrete mixer, the third beneath one of the big-wheeled dumpers. The pair by the mixer were aiming AK-74s; the last guy had exchanged his submachine gun for the grenade launcher.

Halfway up the inclined access strip the Citroën coasted to a stop. Lange scowled. Surely the American wasn't going to trade shots with them from that exposed position? Cautiously, he braked the Opel and climbed out the far side, a Tokarev automatic in his hand.

The Kalashnikovs were hosing lead at the stalled utility. Through the fine rain, Lange saw the glitter of fragmented glass falling from the shattered windows. The car rocked on its springs.

Simultaneously the man with the RPG-7 over his shoulder pressed the trigger on the forward grip. The five-pound grenade leaped from the launch tube, and as the rocket engine cut in and the four stabilizer fins opened, streaked for the target at a speed of nine hundred feet per second, trailing fire.

His aim was hasty. And there was a crosswind blowing rain in gusts over the lot. The grenade fell a couple of yards short and exploded, pulverizing the unmade road and erupting into yellow flame and brown smoke.

The force of the blast was nevertheless enough to blow the Citroën onto its side. For a moment it hung suspended at the road's edge. Then it toppled over and rolled down the steep bank.

Lange was running toward it before the echoes of the crash had died away or the dust had settled. The crumpled Citroën was lying on its back, the roof crushed in, the panels buckled and scarred. One wheel slowly turned.

"Cover me!" Lange shouted to one of the men with a Kalashnikov, beckoning the other forward. Warily, ready to fire at any moment, they drew nearer, separating at last to approach from either side.

Lange dropped to his hands and knees and peered inside the wreck.

The car was empty.

He cursed vehemently in Russian. The son of a bitch must have dived out and rolled down the slope on the far side of the strip just before the Citroën stopped.

But where was he now?

Bolan provided the answer soon enough. A single shot, evidently from a heavy caliber handgun, reverberated around the site. The guy who had fired the RPG-7 dropped facedown to become part of the scenery. The two AK-74 handlers spun around.

Where?

A timekeeper's wooden hut. A gun barrel smashed the window and glass tinkled to the ground. It was now Bolan's lighter weight Beretta that was drilling for blood.

Two 9mm slugs bored into the chest of the man under the concrete mixer, leaving an autorifle on the ground and a dead man gushing blood.

Lange's Tokarev and the remaining Kalashnikov pumped leaden death through the flimsy walls of the hut.

But Bolan had left it for a drainage trench that ran from the foot of the incline, ten yards from the hut, to the turnpike below.

The ceramic pipes had yet to be laid. The Executioner was invisible in the three-foot trench. Lange took refuge behind the overturned Citroën and waved his remaining ally down behind the shovel of a bulldozer.

For a moment the site was silent. Voices drifted on the wind from the turnpike, where motorists had stopped at the upended Skoda and the Renault-Ferrari conflagration.

Again…where the hell was Bolan?

Too late, Lange saw that the RPG-7 and its one spare grenade had vanished from beside the body underneath the dumper. He sprinted from the wreck of the Citroën to an excavation where the ground dropped away.

But the grenade launcher had been taken for another reason. The exit from the site, at the far side of the gas-station shelf, was bounded by a chain link fence with steel-framed wire gates barring the service road. The gates were padlocked with a heavy chain.

The HEAT Missile exploded against them and transformed them into an unrecognizable tangle of twisted metal.

Lange and the man with the AK-74 were on their feet, peppering the trench with nickel-jacketed messengers of extinction.

Once again they were too late. Bolan had already crawled away from the launcher. The next time they heard from him was the most unexpected of all.

A single shot.

Lange's accomplice spun around, clutched his arm and fell. As he and Lange gaped, simultaneously realizing that the gun had been fired from the driving seat of the Opel, which had been left with the passenger door open, the engine roared to life and the vehicle shot away.

Bolan was slouched behind the wheel, his eyes level with the hood as he steered toward the unfinished access road.

Lange fired the Tokarev wildly, but the range—rapidly increasing—was too great for accuracy with a handgun.

Murder in his heart, he watched the Opel curve around the gas-station emplacement, then snake through the shattered gateway onto a country lane. Within two hundred yards, it was lost to sight behind a belt of trees.

Lange was left standing in the rain with an empty pistol, a wounded man and the loss of three cars and five KGB agents to account for.

The undamaged Lada was 150 yards away, but by now the big rock-faced Russian knew better than to attempt a stern chase when Mack Bolan was at the helm.

13

So Lange, the KGB gorilla, had wondered why Mack Bolan should be heading toward Chambéry instead of south, where the action was?

Intel was the answer, the kind that couldn't be fed in through infrared binoculars held by a man in the blister of a Huey Cobra at a height of thirty-two hundred feet.

"There's a place they call the Eagle's Nest," Bolan said to Harry Porrelli, "in the Vercors. It's a kind of an enclosed—"

"I heard of it," Porrelli interrupted. "Just the other day. It seems some crazy Krauts started a chemical factory there, God knows why. What did you want to know, Mack?"

"They tell me this area's a paradise for cavers," Bolan said. "Like, honeycombed with grottoes and connecting tunnels. I want to know if there is any underground way into that valley."

"Personally, I wouldn't know," Porrelli told him. "But there's an old guy in the village used to be a cavers' guide. He could tell you right away. You want to go down there, sink a couple of beers and sound him out?"

"Lead me to him," Bolan said.

Porrelli was an old Army buddy. He was a tall, thin, rangy guy with large, dirty gardener's hands, a tin leg and a shock of white hair. He'd won the leg, the hair and a Purple Heart in a single night during the Tet offensive in Nam.

He married a girl the French left behind when they quit Indochina, and built this two-bedroom frame bungalow on a country road only a few miles from the roadworks site where Bolan had bested Lange and his Russians.

They had a hillside planted with vines, an acre of flatland where Harry grew roses, two cypress trees beside the house, a pond with Muscovy ducks and an electrified fence to keep foxes and other folks' German shepherds away.

It was a good marriage and Bolan hated like hell to co-opt them into his private crusade, but he had nobody else to ask, and Harry had never exactly been a card-carrying Party member!

Bolan junked the Opel by the roadside and they walked the rest of the way to the village. The rain had stopped. Now the clouds withdrew and it was sunny again.

Drinking *pastis* beneath the plane trees in the village square, Porrelli introduced Bolan to a gaunt old man with a white-stubbled chin and a wide, flat Alpine infantryman's beret concealing the fact that his head was completely bald.

The retired guide—his name was Gilbert Vézoul—was one of the few Resistance fighters who had escaped from the Vercors massacre in 1944. At one time he had actually fought with a Maquis formation holed up in the valley they now called the Eagle's Nest, and yes, there was a way, a secret way in. It was possible to enter the valley without using the road tunnel. But it was difficult and dangerous, an underground journey of at least two hours, impossible without a guide.

"A speleologist's route, using underground riverbeds and caverns in the rock?" Bolan asked.

"Yes, *monsieur*."

"I would like very much to be shown that route," Bolan said. "Could I ask you—professionally of course—to act as my guide?"

Vézoul drained his glass and set it carefully on the marble-topped table. He asked simply, "Why?"

Bolan decided to take the two men into his confidence. Briefly, he gave them a rundown on the whole Treynet operation, emphasizing his determination to smash the conspiracy but omitting any mention of the KGB. You never knew how far left some of the wartime partisans might have been.

"Eh bien, s'il s'agit d'une affaire anti-fasciste," Vézoul said, *"je suis d'accord.* If it is a case of fighting the fascists, you can count me in."

"Right," said Bolan. "When do we start?"

Porrelli exchanged glances with the old Resistance fighter. Vézoul nodded. "The entrance to this particular cave system is above Vassieux," Porrelli said. "It's damn near forty miles, and the last part is up a pretty rough mountain track. But there's an old ex-GI jeep in back of the barn at my place. What say we go pick her up right now, while there's still time to make the trip today?"

"We're on our way," Bolan said.

THE STONY TRACK CLIMBED UNEXPECTEDLY to the escarpment from a belt of dense woodland. It was steep and winding, and on some loops the limestone-chip surface was so treacherous that the spinning wheels of the old jeep sent rock fragments showering into the void.

Sometimes the trail lost itself in a barren wilderness of rock webbed with fissures in which clumps of broom and thyme and mastics eked out a meager existence. Twice they had to back up several hundred yards while Vézoul checked his bearings.

But eventually they arrived at a shallow depression floored with coarse mountain grass, beyond which, between two gigantic boulders worn smooth by millenia of rain and snow, was a horizontal opening no more than eighteen inches high.

"This is the way in," Vézoul said. He looked up at the rock face above the boulders. "Your Eagle's Nest is on the far side of the ridge, perhaps a mile in a straight line, maybe less." The weathered features cracked into a smile. "But the route we take is not exactly straight. The passage does, however, become a little higher once we are inside.''

They crawled through the gap, the old man in the lead, Porrelli bringing up the rear. They had come equipped with picks, rope and miners' helmets with inset electric lamps.

After forty or fifty yards of laborious, painful elbow-and-knee work, the passageway opened into a shaft that vanished into the blackness above. "A sinkhole in the ridge," Vézoul explained. The beam of his headlamp swung down. Twenty feet below, the shaft ended on the floor of a huge cavern. "We go that way," he said, uncoiling the rope from around his waist.

They let themselves down. The cavern was immense, the roof and far side lost in the dark even with the combined light of all three lamps.

Several tunnels led off the great rock chamber. Vézoul led them unerringly to a six-foot-long corridor slanting downward. Ducking to avoid the crystalline roof, Bolan followed the guide. Now all around they heard the sounds of water: rushing, gurgling, cascading, dripping.

The tunnel branched, divided again, and they were on a wet ledge that ran above a stream channeled into the rock.

The water frothed and swirled past, hastening toward some secret exit far away. The ledge was narrow and slippery. As they advanced, a distant vibration that seemed to make the rock tremble beneath their feet grew gradually more insistent until finally it was a roar loud enough to make speech impossible. Vézoul motioned the party to stop.

The subterranean stream, wider, deeper and faster now, hurled itself over a step in the limestone and plunged fifty feet into a boiling cauldron of white water that was fed by half a dozen other springs.

The walls had been moist all the way, but now Bolan and his companions were drenched to the skin by the spume flying from these thundering cataracts. The cavern was larger than the first one, the descent more perilous, involving the use of picks, as well as the rope. Once down it was difficult to stay upright; algae and other organisms rendered the uneven surface as slick as melting ice.

He knew that even with the most detailed of charts and the clearest of tape markers, he could never have found his way through this dark labyrinth alone. He was aware, suddenly, of the untold millions of tons of rock above him, of the countless centuries through which, ceaselessly and untiredly, the network of underground rivers had been hollowing out these interconnected passages, eroding away the softer, more soluble parts of the limestone. He shivered.

One day the anthill would collapse.

Not today. Not while there were Treynets to be eroded.

On the far side of the cave they began to climb again. Soon the sound of water was below them. Dark chambers roofed with stalactites opened out to the right and left. Vézoul led them up shaly slopes, along cramped tunnels where they had to bend double, through echoing dark spaces where the light from the lamps was lost.

At last he stopped. They were at the foot of a slanting crevice, a smooth slope of rock down which a current of cool dry air was blowing. "Up there at the top," Vézoul told Bolan. "That is where you come out into your valley. You want to have a look around, we'll wait for you here."

Bolan nodded. He started cautiously to make his way up the slope. When daylight became visible, he switched off his lamp. Five minutes later, he parted a screen of ferns and stared down a rock-strewn incline to the military huts, the parade ground, the pool and the back of the house he had seen from the air.

Rapidly his tactician's eye took in the terrain: cover, angles of attack, points of defense, strength of visible defenders, avenues of safe withdrawal. Long shot, medium shot....

Close-up.

Ten yards away.

Three guys in uniform with Uzi submachine guns, grenades slung from belts, walkie-talkies, field telephones.

Two sat in a sandbagged emplacement; the third walked a regular beat up and down the hillside.

The Treynets knew about the underground passage.

At least, they knew of its existence, they were aware of the possibility that it might be a way in, they took the risk seriously enough to post a permanent guard.

"No way," Bolan said to Porrelli and Vézoul ten minutes later. "One guy, even two or three, wouldn't have a hope in hell of struggling through that crack and making it past the guards alive."

"Not even with grenades?" Porrelli asked.

"Not even with grenades. There's not enough room to make a good throw. And if you lobbed one from the entrance itself, you'd risk blowing your own damned head off, as well as theirs. The guards are too close."

"And so?"

"So it's a dead loss as a means of getting in," Bolan said. "But it would do okay as an emergency exit. You got mobility there, a choice of positions to neutralize those guards, the element of surprise—which you'd never have hauling yourself out through that hole, with earth and stones and waving ferns and all to tip them off."

"But before you get out," Vézoul reminded him gently, "you do have to get in."

Bolan sighed. "Too right," he said. "I'll have to dream up another way."

14

Before he beat his brains out trying to achieve the impossible, Bolan figured it would pay to take a closer look at the ridge surrounding the Eagle's Nest from the side opposite the road tunnel. Porrelli and Gilbert Vézoul came with him the following day.

Approached this way, the escarpment was dwarfed by the long bulk of the Montagne de Lans and the seventy-five-hundred-foot summit of the Grand Veymont behind it. Just the same, it was quite an obstacle, several miles from the nearest highway.

A weed-grown farm track that branched off a minor road beyond Saint-Jean-en-Royans seemed a good bet, but it petered out by a group of gutted buildings that had been left to rot since World War II. After that it was tough going even for Porrelli's jeep.

Because of the watchers that Bolan knew would be on the ridge, they left the jeep in a wood beyond the ruins. From there on down, each man must become part of the scenery.

Vézoul had been a *chasseur alpin*—a soldier with France's elite mountain force. He melted into the background as easily as a jungle leopard in a tree. Porrelli had been a sniper in Vietnam. Like Bolan he was still, despite the tin leg, an ace ground-cover man. The three of them were to make the foot of the escarpment unseen. Porrelli and the old man would then put on an act—two red-necks making a clumsy attempt to hide—an attempt that would draw the attention of the guards while Bolan started the recon that was vital to any future play infiltrating the valley.

"That's the plan, anyway," he told them as they unshipped their gear from the jeep. "But once the whistle blows, each one of us is going to have to play it by ear."

"Just like old times!" Porrelli enthused.

Bolan wore his blacksuit. The others were dressed in hunters' camouflage coveralls. They would pretend they knew that the legal hunting season was over, but there was a nationwide shortage of game; they had heard tell there were hares, snipe, woodcock, maybe even wild boar in the scrub at the foot of the cliff. What harm was there, looking over the terrain? Poachers? No. It wasn't private property, was it?

Each of them carried an old shotgun and an empty game bag. Bolan's shoulder rig housed a shorter-range but more deadly weapon.

From the edge of the wood, the big guy swept the ridge with his binoculars. No sentries were visible, but they would be there, all right. Treynet surrounded himself with professionals.

The question was, how many? And how often did they patrol? Or were they in fixed positions with overlapping fields of view?

Between the wood and the limestone face, the ground rose in hillocks scattered with rock outcrops. Thorn bushes, pistachio, box and an occasional stunted holm oak grew in the crevices.

Bolan and his companions were professionals, too. For them it would not be too hard to make the cliff unobserved, even with other professionals on the alert above. The difficult part came after that.

It was a gray day, heavy and humid. No shadow for cover, but no sunshine either to reflect a telltale gleam from metal or glass.

Deployed over a front of sixty or seventy yards, the three men moved a few feet at a time, worming their way through underbrush, circling in the lee of limestone outliers, crossing the short stretches of open ground only when there was a rival sound or movement that might momentarily distract the attention of a watcher.

A flock of birds, a farm tractor on a distant highway, the sudden barking of a dog, an airplane landing or taking off from the small airfield at Chabeuil in the Rhône valley on the far side of the massif—any of those could be the signal for an abrupt short rush or headlong plunge.

He had allowed ninety minutes for the advance from the wood to the cliff face. By the time they made it, each man was scratched, grazed, bruised, drenched in sweat, his hands and knees lacerated from contact with the rocky terrain.

A short distance from the face, Bolan came on a simple three-strand wire fence. It was unlikely that Treynet would risk legal action by electrifying an outside boundary, but he crawled supercarefully beneath it just the same. At intervals of a hundred yards, white lettering on red notice boards shouted, Private Property! No Entry!

Ten yards inside the boundary fence a larger board carried a harsh message.

YOU HAVE BEEN WARNED!

An important research installation is located on this private property. The perimeter is patrolled by guard dogs. Trespassers advance beyond this point at their own risk.

Bolan grinned. Sure. But the risk, he hoped, would turn out in the end to be Treynet's. He continued on.

"You are being very foolish!" a disembodied voice said from behind a boulder to his right. "You have already been warned twice. Get out while you can. Anything that happens to you now is entirely your own responsibility."

Bolan started. His hand flashed involuntarily toward the silenced Beretta 93-R in its shoulder rig. But the voice was mechanical. The words were recorded on a tape loop. He must have broken an electronic beam someplace and actuated the recorder.

He crawled around the rock. Yeah, sure enough, there it was, a small plastic box with a speaker grill cemented into a hollow. One wire ran behind him to wherever the sensor was, another disappeared into the ground in the direction of the cliff.

Bolan swore. For sure that indicated that each time the tape was actuated a warning light or bell or the like would flash somewhere above.

Already the guards would know there were strangers around.

He whistled three times—the signal to start to play poacher.

He hoped the alarm would not pinpoint the location of the actuated sensor. If it did, they would know the poachers were not alone.

At the foot of the escarpment, Bolan searched warily for trip wires, electronic eyes and miniature radar devices.

He found none, but that did not mean there weren't any there. The *garrigue*—that thorny mixture of shrubs, grasses, thistles and aromatic herbs growing around the limestone outcrops of southern France—was probably used to conceal such traps.

He looked along the foot of the escarpment. Porrelli and Vézoul were skulking behind a great slab of rock that hid them from anyone at ground level but left them totally exposed to anyone directly above. Bolan smiled. They were playing their parts well.

There were no visible paths climbing the cliff face, but the weathered and eroded rock, seamed with fissures and studded with clumps of evergreen, would present no problem to an experienced climber.

The first hint that one was descending came in the form of a dislodged stone that bounced from crag to crag between Bolan and his friends.

From beneath a leafy bush, he peered upward. Two uniformed guards were traversing a shelf that slanted down toward Porrelli and the old man. They carried the favorite tool of the French hunter, the 3-barreled sporting gun: two chambers for 12-bore shells filled with heavy-gauge shot; one rifled barrel for .500 express slugs.

Good hunters looked down on them as unsporting, sitting-duck arms, though the .500 express could be reassuring if one were facing an enraged boar. As a choice for Treynet's guards, Bolan had to admit it was smart.

Intruders gunned down with an Uzi or a Kalashnikov would be hard to explain away before the local law. Awkward questions would be asked. But with one of these weapons the argument could be believable. "It was desolated. We were out shooting on our own property. The guy must have been a trespasser. We didn't see him.... A hunting accident, a most regrettable accident...."

The guards shouted something at the two supposed poachers. Bolan didn't hear whether they replied.

And he didn't hear the dog until it was ten yards away.

It was a Doberman pinscher. A tall, black, muscled brute with slavering jaws and eyes red with inbred hate. Bounding over the rocky scrub, it leaped for him, snarling, without breaking its stride.

Bolan barely had time to bring up the Beretta, steady his aim and pull the trigger.

A 3-round burst from the silenced automatic smashed into the dog's chest, stopping it in midair. It fell dead at Bolan's feet. He lowered the gun regretfully. It was a beautiful beast, but it was evil. It had purposely been turned into a superbly tuned killing machine.

A second Doberman approached him silently from behind and knocked him forward to the ground. As he rolled onto his back, trying to regain his breath, the animal jumped him again, planting its front feet on his chest, pinning him down.

The lethal fangs were inches from his throat. The dog's hot saliva dribbled onto his skin, its fetid breath playing over him.

From above came a shout. The Dobermans' handler was near. Bolan thought fast. The beast was trained to keep him immobilized until the handler arrived. He must act decisively now or be lost.

But how?

His gun arm was twisted beneath him; he was lying on the weapon. If he made any move to free it, the killer dog would rip out his throat. If he allowed himself to stay pinned, he would be at the mercy of the approaching guard.

With infinite care beneath the ferocious glare, he inched his free hand down toward the broad-bladed commando knife strapped in the heel of his left boot.

He stretched his fingers. He couldn't touch the knife.

Very slowly he flexed his knee, drawing the foot toward his hand. Sensing the muscles tense beneath the blacksuit, the Doberman growled warningly. Bolan froze.

Again the handler shouted, now from just beyond a rock overhang much nearer. Pebbles cascaded from above and plunged into a clump of coarse grass. The dog barked once in answer.

Bolan touched the hilt of the knife, clenched his fingers around it. He slid the knife from its sheath.

If he was to get away with it, his move must be swift, positive, accurate—and deadly.

Otherwise, better not even think about it.

For a third time the handler called.

The dog lifted its head to bark.

Now.

All Bolan's formidable strength and all his will went into the complex movement. The hand with the knife flashed upward. The blade sliced between two ribs to pierce the heart. Bolan slid from beneath the dog.

The Doberman howled.

Its teeth snapped frenziedly near Bolan's throat but the animal was dead before the powerful jaws could close. He shoved the weight away and scrambled to his feet as thick blood spurted over him.

He was standing beneath the overhang when the uniformed handler jumped down, eyes flicking left, right, shotgun at the ready.

Bolan sent him after his dogs with two 9mm skylights to ventilate his skull.

The two guards farther along the escarpment had reached ground level and were questioning Porrelli and Vézoul, their backs turned to the Executioner. Evidently they had heard nothing.

Bolan began tracing the handler's steps upward. He climbed fast, the lower part of the cliff not being too difficult, and had progressed almost fifty feet when, groping for a handhold, he touched a hidden wire.

It was designed as a preliminary warning, he guessed. He didn't see what mechanism was used, but he heard the noise in time to draw back into a narrow traverse before a large chunk of limestone, then several boulders each the size of his head, plunged past down the rock face to crash into the *garrigue* below.

He found another hidden wire twenty feet higher, and traced it to a small pressurized fuel tank attached to an ignition device and a flamethrowing nozzle. Very neat. If the intruder was not incinerated, the blaze would alight the tinder growing on the escarpment and tip off the guards that a stranger was prowling.

The third wire was the simplest. Depressing it withdrew the pin from a grenade and released it down the cliff to explode precisely where the clumsy foot had tripped the wire.

Bolan crouched behind a limestone outcropping, hanging on with one arm and covering his face with the other as the small bomb burst with a cracking detonation. Rock chips stung him. When the fragments stopped falling, he looked up.

Two hundred feet above, three guards alerted by the explosion stood at the cliff edge, visible in silhouette. The flat bang of large-bore shotguns punctured the air, followed by the sharper crack made by some kind of automatic. Lead shot peppered the limestone and a heavy-caliber slug gouged a furrow into the projection sheltering Bolan, then whined off into space.

Bolan, untouched, emerged from behind the rock and emptied the Beretta's magazine. But firing vertically upward at that range was more a gesture than a menace.

He ducked back and reloaded with a fresh 15-round box. The men above fired again. Bolan replied. This time one of the guards jerked abruptly upright and disappeared. His companions withdrew.

Bolan scrambled back down the cliff.

He had never intended to penetrate the valley today, only to test the strength of the defenses on this side of the massif, to see if it was possible.

Well, okay, they had been tested.

And it was not possible.

As he had feared, the chances of a single person climbing the ridge and making the valley beyond were nil. That was by daylight; as for a night ascent...

No way.

He turned toward the outcrop where he had last seen Vézoul and Harry Porrelli. There had been two sharp reports, followed by a shout and then a single shot. Keeping as close to the foot of the escarpment as possible, Bolan ran to his friends.

One of the guards lay with outflung arms in the center of a spreading web of scarlet, which had already reached a crevice and was dripping down over the thorns and thistles below. What had been his face was now a gory mask.

The other man was draped facedown over a small pinnacle, splinters of bone piercing through the bloodied ruin of his back.

Believing themselves to be dealing only with hick trappers, the two guards had incautiously allowed their attention to wander when they heard the shooting from Bolan's sector.

The mistake had cost them their lives.

Waiting for Bolan to rejoin them, the "trappers" had exchanged their 12-bores for the expensive 3-barrel sportguns.

The Executioner and his allies returned to the jeep. There was no more fire from the men on the cliff.

They passed the Dobermans and the handler Bolan had killed. Vézoul contemplated the two holes drilled in the man's forehead. "Could be awkward," he said, "if anyone happened to have seen us on the way."

Deliberately he raised his newly acquired weapon and fired two charges of buckshot into the dead man's face. The bullet holes disappeared. So did most of the face.

"A hunting accident," Vézoul said, clucking and shaking his head. "Folks should really be more careful the way they handle guns."

"Strike two," Porrelli said when they reached the jeep. "It's not gonna be three and out, is it?"

"Not on your life," Bolan replied, gazing upward through the trees. "Not on your goddamn life!" he repeated excitedly.

Porrelli and Vézoul stared at him. "Look!" Bolan yelled. "Up there! There's your blueprint for a night entry unobserved!"

Between the branches, over the distant shoulder of the Grand Veymont, three tiny triangles sailed in silhouette against the overcast sky. Lower down, a fourth spiraled slowly toward a belt of woodland and then soared.

Hang gliders.

15

At the hang-gliding school in Saint-Pierre-de-Chartreuse, Porrelli insisted they get a two-man trainer with ski-lift-style tandem seats. "Because if you think I'm gonna let you go in there alone, Mack, you're out of your mind."

Bolan shook his head. "No way, old buddy. No way. You got a wife and a flower farm to look after, a kid in high school, and—"

"Bullshit. I'm seeing the world collapse around me here in France." Porrelli pointed to a newspaper lying on a desk in the school's front office. A bomb had been thrown into a crowded bar in Orléans and fifteen people were dead; three hostages had been killed in a holdup; the phrase "crime wave" screamed from the front page. "You say you know who's organizing this shit, and why," he continued. "And you tell me you're gonna go in there and do something about it. What the hell makes you think you can leave me out now?"

"Listen, Harry, I needed your help with the caves. I'm grateful for that. I'll need it again when I quit that valley. But I'm not—"

"You listen to me," Porrelli said earnestly. He glanced over his shoulder. Her back turned, the clerk was at her desk, readying papers for Bolan to sign. "I mean *listen*. Back there in Nam, we were fighting for something, right? We had a purpose?"

"Sure we did."

"We didn't kid ourselves we were fighting for a better world maybe, but we were part of a good world and we wanted to keep it that way, right?"

"Right, Harry. And so?"

"So it was kind of a duty to go in there and do what we could once we had seen the way things were going." Porrelli gestured helplessly. "I'm not explaining myself good, Mack, but—"

"You're doing all right."

"Well, I mean it's the same kind of thing here, ain't it? Here's these SOBs, you know, fucking up the good life for everyone, like the Mafia back home. I heard tell you fought pretty good against those bastards. Well, this is a kind of a Mafia routine, too, only it happens to be political. And you're going in there again and put a stop to it, right?"

"I'm going to do my damnedest."

"Okay, so if I don't know nothing about it, in you go and the best of luck, Jack. But I do know about it. I can't unknow what you told me. The way I see it, once I'm wise to the situation, I reckon I have a duty to go in there with you and help all I can."

Seeing that Bolan still looked dubious, Porrelli went on. "So that Jean-Paul can stay in that high school in Chambéry. So that the wife can go pick roses without some teenage hoodlum throws her skirt over her head and tries to rape her. So I can take time off to make the Paris flower show without fearing my house has been burned down while I'm gone."

"I don't know, Harry."

"For God's sake, Mack, with all the shit they're gonna throw at you in there you're gonna need backup. You want someone riding shotgun while you go in and do what you have to do."

For an instant longer Bolan hesitated. He hated like hell to get a family man mixed up in his crusade. But what the guy said was true. All of it.

He reached out and shook his old buddy's hand. "You're on." And then to the girl, "Make that a dual, honey." He turned back to Porrelli. "As if I didn't have enough on my plate, now I'm lumbered with a passenger!"

Porrelli grinned happily. "Think again, buster," he said. "I fly those things pretty good. You can leave the piloting to me while you shoot the opposition down in flames."

When the wing was packed into its tarp and strapped down on the roof rack of Porrelli's Citroën, Bolan said curiously, "How come you made yourself into a fly-boy, Harry? I always had you figured as a ground-cover guy. I mean, even back there in Nam as a sniper, you said you were better off beneath a bush than up in some tree."

Porrelli laughed. "Happened this way. What I was doing, I was down there in Provence, gone down to Aix to visit with my brother-in-law Raoul to learn about raising vines. Roses I knew, from my old man's place back in the Shenandoah, but vines is something else. Well, one day, waiting for the damn things to show above the earth, what I was doing, I was filling in my time taking the pickup to Valence to get some stuff Raoul had ordered, when ten miles from anywhere I came on this cute little convertible pulled way over on the shoulder and this pretty girl looking up into the air."

He shook his head, still smilng. "It was the damnedest thing! I stop to chat her up, ask whether maybe the heap had died on her or what, and before I get to first base this guy drops down from out of the sky beneath this kite rig—and she's been waiting for him to show all the time!"

Porrelli shrugged. "Don't know why, but I was hooked right off. I thought, that's a hell of a way for a dude to make a date with his girl. And I checked up on it, and I learned. For a while back there, just for kicks, I used to fly from here down to our place right around teatime, and surprise Marie-Louise and the kid. You know, Superman from the sky!" He sighed. "Don't seem to be able to find the time for it anymore, but I ain't forgot."

"Rusty or not," Bolan said, "a copilot I could use. You got connections in the explosives business, too, Harry?"

"Explosives?"

"When I get into this place, there's going to be things I want to liquidate—drug stocks, arms, records maybe. I don't know. But I have to be prepared."

Porrelli shook his head. "Vézoul," he said. "He's the guy you want. His brother-in-law's a quarryman over the other side of Chambéry."

"You figure he could chisel the guy out of a couple of kilos of plastique?"

"Listen, if it's a question of zapping the Fascists, Gilbert could get you anything from a second-hand Sherman tank to a SAM."

"Swell," Bolan said. "We're going to need him anyway when it's all over, to wait at the mouth of that passage in the rock and lead us back to civilization through all those galleries."

"No problem. He'll only be sore there ain't no such thing as a three-seat delta wing!" Porrelli drove out of the school and turned left along the road for Chambéry. "What say we go spoil his siesta and take him over to pay a surprise visit on his brother-in-law right now?"

"Suits me," Bolan said. From the stepped-up terror campaign reported by the newspapers and fragments of conversation overheard between Lange and Strakhov, he had the impression that something big was brewing, that the KGB spymaster was pushing the Treynets and their slaves toward some action from which there would be no drawing back. Some hellish deal that would nudge the country one step further into total anarchy.

Bolan aimed to get in there and wreck that plan before it was off the ground. "There's a three-quarter moon," he said. "Know what time she rises?"

"Around nine or ten after nine tonight and tomorrow," Porrelli said.

Bolan paused. He was aware of the perils of night time hang gliding—lack of air currents and thermals—but he had no choice.

"I'd like for us to be airborne just before, but I'll need the moonlight to locate the valley and know where to put down."

"But not so high and bright that they'll see us coming. Gilbert can help there, too. He'll wise you up on the best spot to take off from. Somewhere high enough to give us a run-in but near enough to the escarpment so we won't be up there too long."

"Yeah," Bolan said soberly. "It's on the ground that we'll need to spend the time."

GILBERT VÉZOUL'S BROTHER-IN-LAW CAME ACROSS with a dozen small packs of HMX late that day. The next morning Bolan bought a stack of cheap wristwatches at a Chambéry supermarket, then made certain modifications involving batteries, wire, electrical terminals and steel draftsman's pins.

He removed the hour hand from one watch, pierced the plastic dome with a pin to which wire had been attached, linked it to a battery and one of the detonators supplied by the friendly quarryman, then pushed the detonator into a stick of HMX. He repeated the procedure with the other watches.

To prime the delayed-action bomb, it was necessary only to wind the watch and set the minute hand anything short of an hour away from the pin. When hand and pin touched, the circuit would be completed and the plastique would explode.

That afternoon they took the jeep and checked out the take-off area Vézoul favored on the eastern slopes of the Grand Veymont.

Although it meant a longer flight, the thermal current rising from the Isère Valley would be far stronger than anything they could expect from the high Vercors plateau, the old man explained.

Just before dusk they left the jeep below a hundred-foot vertical cliff and carried the components of the glider up a path that snaked around to the flat rock they were to use. Once they were airborne, Vézoul would drive back to Vassieux, leave the utility by the entrance to the cave system, and journey through the galleries to the Eagle's Nest exit, to be there to guide them back when the raid was over.

Bolan was stretching the sail over the wing's A-frame spars. "One thing, Harry," he said. "It sure as hell is good to have you with me. But it's going to be rugged down there. It could be terminal. I can't guarantee we'll be there to meet Gilbert. I can't promise a safe exit. If you want to change your mind and go wait with him, I won't think any the worse—"

"Save your breath, General," Porrelli cut in brusquely. "I volunteered for this detail, remember?"

16

The rough slant of limestone on which they had assembled the glider gave Bolan and Porrelli a fair run; below was nothing but the sheer cliff, and at the foot of it was the jeep.

A cool breeze blew down from the Alpine peaks to the east. Beyond them the darkness was paling. The moon would be rising any minute.

Porrelli was carrying an old Webley pistol and the 3-barreled sporting gun he had taken from the dead guard at the Eagle's Nest two days before. It was a beautifully crafted Venere Extralusso made by the Italian firm of Abbiatico Salvinelli. Canvas pouches filled with the delayed-action charges were attached to his belt and, like Bolan, he had fifty rounds of spare ammunition.

Bolan himself toted Big Thunder on his right hip, the silenced Beretta in its shoulder rig, Konzaki's infrared binoculars on a strap around his neck, and a flat but powerful electric torch and a tiny Minox camera in pockets in his blacksuit.

Heavier artillery, he reckoned, could be lifted from the defenders if necessary. Initially, the important thing was not to get loaded down with gear.

The two men harnessed up. Bolan reached for the spars, nodded to Porrelli and said, "Okay, we're on our way." He gave a thumbs-up to Vézoul. "See you later, *cher ami*."

They ran lightly down the rock-strewn slope and allowed the thermal current climbing the cliff face to fill the sail and buoy them up over the edge.

Bolan was no world champion but he had some experience with delta wings. He had taken a course when the sport first became a big deal, and had kept in shape as part of the tough training routine he imposed on himself during the Stony Man era.

Yet every time he lifted off he was knocked out afresh by the magic of hang gliding, by the intoxicating sense of total freedom in flight.

Yeah, maybe if everyone could feel this way, could do this thing and share this drifting joy, the human prospect could get to look more pleasing, too.

Maybe.

Right now, it did not seem too hot a bet. The Executioner was on his way to eradicate a little more of the vileness.

He wheeled into the breeze fifty feet away from the cliff, settling into the double-concave seat, checking out his harness and lines. The night wind numbed his face, drying the tears blown from the corners of his eyes across his cheekbones. Beyond the distant summits a rim of moon hoisted itself into the dark sky and made the river twisting below a thread of beaten gold.

Bolan looked back. Behind the flank of the mountain the crest of the Eagle's Nest ridge was also limned in gold. As the glider winged toward it, he could make out the contours of the Treynet stronghold.

He wheeled once more, Porrelli silent beside him, breaking the turn halfway through to sail downwind across the northern slope of the Grand Veymont and sample the air on the lee side.

Five minutes later, buffeted in a patch of turbulence, he pulled back the control bar to gain speed, then dropped the nose and veered again into the wind, floating downward parallel to the ridge.

He was maybe two hundred feet above the crest and a quarter of a mile away from it. It was tough to estimate. He had to be high enough to carry them over the top, but low enough not to be forced into a spiraling descent over the valley, where the wing would be a signal of impending danger and a moving target for Treynet's men.

Bolan reckoned the highest concentration of guards would be above the road tunnel. He aimed to circle around the valley and land between the cave and the rock face where he had been attacked by the dogs.

Banking over the ridge, he saw the house, the parade ground and the factory beyond. The moon was a luminous disk hanging above the jagged peaks behind them. "Hold tight, Harry," he said quietly. "I'm going in now."

He put the nose down hard, swooping toward the cliff face in a long shallow dive, dropping momentarily below the crest to swing back hard into the wind, the trailing edge of the wing fluttering as the glider neared stalling speed. Then they planed over the lip of the escarpment a bare ten feet above the rock.

Treetops came toward them like the dark waves of some angry sea as they skimmed the head of the valley. There was more turbulence here; as though it was adrift on an ocean swell, the wing lifted weightlessly, then dropped into the troughs of the gusting breeze.

Bolan followed the slope down beyond the wood, gliding to a clearing perhaps two hundred feet above and five hundred yards away from the nearest building. At the last moment he ended the flight by turning yet again into the wind, allowing the sail's trailing edge to flap like the jib of a dinghy, shoving the nose down to run over tussocks of rough grass as the rest of the air spilled from the wing.

Before they started to dismantle, Bolan heard voices, a rustle in the undergrowth. The noises came from the edge of the wood sixty or seventy yards behind them.

He bit his lip. He had reckoned on an undetected landing. He had hoped to make the buildings below before any guard even suspected intruders were around.

If the defenders were tipped off now, the raid would be ten times tougher to enact. They could floodlight the place, alert all the personnel from the barrack huts, call their dogs up from below.

He dropped down among the grass clumps and pulled Porrelli with him. "Leave this to me," he whispered. "Don't make a sound." He unleathered the Beretta, pulled back the slide.

Anyone stumbling upon them this early must be liquidated. Quickly. Silently. Before any reports went back to base.

The voices were nearer now. Branches moved.

"You're crazy. What could there be in the sky up here at night?"

"I tell you I heard something. A kind of fluttering, a flapping. It was over this way."

"A fox. A badger. Like I say, we disturbed some roosting bird."

"It weren't that kind of a flap. More like a sailboat or somethin'."

"Now I know you're out of your skull! Shit, man—sailboats in the sky? Ain't no water for fifteen mile anyhow."

"There *was* somethin', Leon. Up there. I didn't see it too clearly, but I kind of thought some dark shape...I felt wind on my face."

"The only wind here's up your goddamned ass. Because you're full of shit, Pinter, that's what. Now let's for Chrissake—"

"I think we should look around."

The two men walked out from beneath the trees. Bolan could distinguish their dim shapes on the moonlit slope. They were still arguing.

"We're wastin' our time," the man called Leon growled. "If there was anythin' screwball..."

They had discovered the hang glider, looking in the wan half light like some monstrous fish beached on a lunar shore.

"Hell!" Pinter shouted. "I told you. Didn't I tell—"

The sentence was never finished. Resting on his elbows, Bolan unfolded the foregrip, held the Beretta in both hands, aimed carefully and squeezed the trigger.

The gun grunted once, bucking in his grasp.

Instantly, overlaying it like a second shot, came the sound of the 9mm slug sledgehammering into Pinter's chest, choking the breath from his lungs. He folded forward, dead before he hit the ground.

Leon cried out. The flash-hider on the Beretta had kept Bolan's position a secret. There was a faint slithering sound that the Executioner recognized: a walkie-talkie aerial being extended.

Bolan was kneeling in the grass, the electric torch in his left hand. The bright beam penetrated the night, spotlighting the remaining guard. The transceiver was against his lips, and he was about to speak.

Bolan shot the radio from his hands. The guy moved convulsively toward his shotgun. Before he could bring it up, a 3-round burst from the silenced 93-R blew the lower half of his face away. He fell from the light and lay still.

Bolan scrambled to the glider; Porrelli limped after him, the tin leg rattling against a rock in the grass. "You want to dismantle now?" he called in a low voice.

"Uh-uh. We have to get out of here," Bolan replied. "We'll stash these two in the bushes and drag the wing up to the trees. But after that we're on our way."

There was a sudden lightness, a relief almost, a relaxation of tension in his manner as he added, "Whether or not these two are missed, we're over the top and into the enemy lines now, Harry!"

BEFORE HE STEERED PORRELLI's JEEP back up to Vassieux and the cave entrance, Gilbert Vézoul had four or five miles to cover along a minor road that paralleled the valley floor. Not far from Monestier-de-Clermont, he pulled over onto the shoulder outside a country inn.

Around the building was a big lamplit beer garden, with chairs and tables beneath orchard trees. And all over the garden and road and a huge adjacent parking lot, hundreds, perhaps thousands, of young bikers yelled and laughed and sang.

The roadside parking lot and parts of the garden were jammed with motorcycles—big 4-cylinder Yamahas, Kawasakis, Hondas, smaller BMWs and trials machines; 250cc and 150cc lightweights, mopeds, even a prewar Norton and a collector's prize, a mint example of a Vincent Black Prince.

The kids came in all sizes and all styles: longhairs, skinheads, punks with flaming cockatoo cuts, hard rockers, mods. Their gear varied from faded jeans through junk-store cast-offs to brass-studded leathers, the girls as well as the boys.

Vézoul saw yellow-and-black posters pasted to the plane trees lining the route.

JETs JETs JETs JETs
TOUR-de-FRANCE
NATIONWIDE
MOTO-RALLY
Départ: La Trinité
Thurs. May 7, 0900

The old Resistance fighter lingered several minutes with the engine idling. Nobody took any notice. Finally, since the road showed no signs of clearing and he still had a half-hour drive before he started the long journey through the caves, he sounded the horn in short bursts.

Still the crowd in front of him made no attempt to disperse. Vézoul leaned on the button, edging the jeep forward in first.

Reluctantly some of the bikers drew back. Some shouted at him, some jeered, others remained mulishly in his way, forcing him to steer a zigzag course between different sections of the throng. In the parking lot, bands of riders were kickstarting their machines, gunning the engines, walking them out onto the roadway, ready to ride away along the route Vézoul had just traversed. The noise was indescribable.

At last only one small group barred the road. There were four of them, two already astride their powerful machines, the others leaning insolently against their saddles with arms folded. Behind one of the riders a girl was perched on the pillion seat.

Most of the bikers were anonymous beneath visored helmets, but these four youths sported Nazi-style caps with black mackintosh covers and shiny peaks. They were dressed in black leather studded with metal and their tunics were decorated with German iron crosses and SS insignia. One wore a red armband with a swastika in a white circle.

Vézoul leaned out from behind the jeep's windshield and shouted above the bellow of exhausts. "Let me pass, will you? I don't have all night to waste."

The young man with the armband pushed himself upright and walked deliberately over. He was a little older than the others, maybe twenty-five, with a two-day stubble shadowing his fleshy jaw. He stood with one jackbooted foot planted on the jeep's running board and spit into the dust. "Just who the fuck did you think you was speakin' to, granddad?" he inquired.

"I asked you to get out of the way," Vézoul said. "I've already been held up almost ten minutes."

"Ten minutes! Well, now ain't that just too bad," the biker drawled. "But you know somethin', granddad? I always thought this was like a free country. Know what I mean? And in my book that means we got just as much right as you to be on this motherfuckin' road. More maybe, 'cause we're still alive and you look like you shoulda been below ground years ago.''

"To be on it, but not to block it," Vézoul said shortly.

The girl and the three other riders were giggling. "Who's blocking the road?" the biker said with mock innocence. He glanced over his shoulder and winked at his companions. "You can always walk, old-timer. Plenty of room for a pedestrian, even a beat-up old shit like you. I told you—it's a free country."

Vézoul lost his temper.

"You dare to talk about a free country? You?" He pointed at the swastika. "When you have the insolence to parade in that filth? When your brainless, gutter-bred friends think it smart to flaunt those badges of dishonor? If it wasn't for beat-up old shits like me and the comrades who died fighting for that freedom, you and your kind would be slave laborers someplace in central Europe today...and then you'd bloody well know what that swastika stood for!"

He stomped the pedal and the jeep surged forward, throwing the biker off-balance. Vézoul steered the vehicle across the shoulder, knocked over a table and three chairs, skated back onto the road and accelerated away in a cloud of dust.

They caught up with him a mile farther on.

The four bikes roared alongside, crowding the jeep, forcing Vézoul onto the verge, cutting in ahead so that he had to stop.

They kicked their machines onto their stands and strode back to the jeep. The old man sat gripping the metal wheel. There were no windows to wind up, no doors to lock.

"I'll tell *you* somethin', granddad," the guy with the armband said. "It just so happens I don't go for bein' knocked off my feet on a public highway. It just so happens we don't like bein' insulted in public. We don't like bein' told what we can wear and what we can't wear. We don't like bein' taken for shitheads, especially by some asshole who's lucky he ain't in the grave already."

"Maybe we should help the old bastard on his way some?" another youth said with a sneer.

"Naw. Better we should teach him a lesson so he don't risk makin' the same mistake again," yet another suggested.

"Yeah," agreed a fourth. "We wouldn't want an old guy like that, a patriot who fought for his country an' all, to foul up his social life, would we? Hey, Saul. What say we start in with the reeducation program right now?"

"I think you got somethin' there," the rider with the armband said. He reached in suddenly, grabbed Vézoul's collar with both hands and hauled him from the jeep.

They stood around him in the light of the headlamps. One of them snatched off the *chasseur alpin* beret. "Why, Baldy," he yelled, "whatever happened to the hair, man?"

"He gave his hair for his country!" Saul guffawed.

Vézoul said nothing. He was a brave man, but he was old.

"Lesson One," Saul said. "We don't like folks what are disrespectful about our gear." His arms shot out to push Vézoul violently away from him. The old man staggered, stumbled, almost fell, but was checked by another youth.

"Lesson Two," the next biker said. "We don't like our intelligence insulted." In his turn he shoved Vézoul savagely away.

"Especially in front of a lady," said the third, sending the old man reeling.

"That's right," Saul said. "Hold him, you guys. Maybe Corinne should have the right to a little schoolteachin' herself. Here, try your aim, honey."

Corinne had dismounted and was standing just outside the circle. She was a skinny girl with an overpainted face and blond hair tied back in a ponytail. She wore a one-piece leather coverall and high-heeled black boots with pointed toes.

Now she stepped forward as two of the bikers seized Vézoul's arms and held him upright. Saul and the fourth man trod hard on his feet so that he was immobilized with his legs spread.

Corinne smiled. She drew back her leg and kicked Vézoul hard in the crotch.

The old man gave an animal cry. His body convulsed,
trying to jackknife forward, but the bikers held him fast.
They were laughing. "Maybe he didn't understand so
good," Saul said, leering. "Teach him again, Corinne."

Once more the pointed toe sank with agonizing force into
Vézoul's testicles. Simultaneously Saul swung a gauntleted
fist and slammed a vicious blow to the pit of the captive's
stomach. "Teach you not to talk out of turn, you bastard!" he snarled.

The youths relaxed their grasp and Vézoul doubled up,
vomiting. They started punching them, the arms rising and
falling rhythmically.

"That's right, give it to him!" Corinne cried shrilly.
"Beat the shit out of the old man!"

Soon the bastard's strangled cries ceased.

For a while there was no sound but the scrape of feet on
the macadam, the panting of breath, the thud of fists on
flesh. Once, sickeningly, there was an unmistakable splintering of bone.

Vézoul lay on his back in the headlamp glare. Twin
streams of scarlet ran from his smashed nose. Blood soaked
his shirt and pants. One eye was closed, his lips were split
and there were lacerations all over his bare scalp.

They pushed the jeep over onto its side, unscrewed the gas
tank and ignited it. They whooped and jumped around the
fire, laughing hysterically. Then they remounted and roared
back toward the inn.

As the flame danced and eventually died down, Vézoul
lay choking in the ditch, drowning in the blood from his
own internal hemorrhages.

17

Philip Swanton was tall and thin, a sallow-faced forty-year-old with a long jaw, a thin blade of a nose, and straight, black lusterless hair. He sat fingering his wineglass as the four other men around the dining table discussed the smuggling of terrorist arms into France.

Swanton was interested in the conversation for two mutually exclusive reasons: one professional, because he had been seconded from the Central Foreign Bureau to Narcotics; the other private because...well, because Philip Swanton was a guy on the make.

Most of the talking tonight came from Schmitt-Heinkel and Lange, the two Germans sitting on his right. Jacques Edouard Treynet, across the candlelit table, contented himself with an occasional question. Jules, his father, florid and overweight with a shock of white hair, smiled from the head of the table and made appreciative murmurs now and then. The girl, Eliane Falcoz, took no part in the discussion.

Let her clam up. Interpol or no Interpol, Philip Swanton would have news for her later. The toffee-nosed little bitch would have something to say then all right. She would have to try to talk her way out of the corner he'd trapped her into. Swanton would enjoy that.

"The length, it is less than nine inches," Schmitt-Heinkel was saying. "The length makes the Ingram MAC-11 ideal for covert activity, as I believe one or two of your clients have discovered already. For holdups, plane hijacks, that kind of thing, a machine pistol that hides beneath the jacket is not to be sneered at.''

He swirled the wine around in his glass and sipped appreciatively. He was drinking a pale gold Johannisberger Erntebringer, everybody else was on claret. He turned to Jacques Edouard Treynet. ''As you know, two or three years ago the American administration forbade the manufacturers, the Military Armaments Corporation of Marietta, Georgia, to export the weapon. It was obviously the perfect tool for subversives.''

The German drained his glass and reached for the slender bottle. ''You, sir—'' he turned to the elder Treynet ''—will doubtless know that more than two hundred of the guns had already been sold to private-arms dealers. And that the U.S. Treasury Department managed to locate and seize one hundred thirty of these. You may be aware that the remaining seventy were illegally smuggled to the Middle East by Iraqi officials abusing their diplomatic immunity. And that these found their way into the hands of the Palestinians.''

Again Schmitt-Heinkel paused. Finally he added impressively, ''What you will not know is that fifty of those seized have—how shall I put it?—have reemerged recently from state custody.'' Another pause. ''Gentlemen, I have the means to acquire those guns.''

''How soon...and how much?'' the younger Treynet asked.

''Within a week. I have my sources. As to the price, I am able, because of my contacts, to offer them at the very competitive figure of seven hundred fifty dollars apiece. Inclusive of two hundred rounds of ammunition.''

''Take them,'' Julies Treynet said to his son. ''With the elections in less than a month and tomorrow's distribution to come, they will be invaluable.''

''A small supplementary payment will also be necessary,'' Schmitt-Heinkel said smoothly. ''Perhaps two thousand dollars. This is simply to ensure that certain American officials look, shall we say, the other way at the vital moment. As Herr Swanton will know, when seized goods—narcotics in particular—find their way back into the market, certain machinery has inevitably to be...greased.''

Herr Swanton knew only too well, and he had a numbered bank account in Geneva to prove it.

Since he had talked himself into a directorship of the chemical company as part of his CFB work, the glamour of the Treynets' high-finance existence had seduced him away from his duty. The cover had become more desirable than the secret identity it was designed to conceal.

Swanton had every intention now of tipping off the Treynets that they were under Interpol and Narcotics Bureau observation. But first the girl must be disposed of.

Well, that was not going to be too difficult. Not with the information he had. He would not even have to fix it himself. In any case, it would be a pleasure watching the bitch go down. A broad who turned thumbs-down on Philip Swanton and stayed next to young Treynet deserved what was coming to her.

And, with luck, when she went she would take that son of a bitch Mack Bolan with her.

''Is the merchandise ready for distribution when the rally starts tomorrow morning?'' Jules Treynet asked.

''Yes, father, of course.'' The son sounded irritated. ''You know everything is under control, as always. The consignments are docketed and waiting in Dispatch, the riders have their numbers and their routes, even the individual sachets have identification codes.''

''Excellent. And the...manifestations...will take place as arranged, before the elections? Long enough before for the country to be in chaos, and long enough after the distribution for our voters to be crying out for a fresh supply?''

''Don't *worry*,'' Jacques Edouard Treynet said. ''I told you.''

''The schedule is already drawn up,'' Lange said. ''Banks, subpost offices, supermarkets, department stores for the holdups, and railroad stations, air terminals, shopping precincts for the bombs. Callers representing a dozen different subversive groups will telephone claiming responsibility for the attacks. Chaos you will have.''

Schmitt-Heinkel chuckled. ''Even this mercenary Bolan has unwittingly played into our hands. Your own dead soldiers in Paris, the unexplained auto-route deaths and the bodies on the roadworks site near Chambéry—all of them add to the atmosphere of unease.''

''Just the same,'' the younger Treynet said, ''I would prefer it, I would feel happier, if this troublesome fellow could be eliminated once for all before Operation Rally is under way. Can I rely on you gentlemen?''

''Don't you worry,'' Lange said grimly. ''We are working on it.''

NOT HARD ENOUGH, the troublesome fellow thought to himself. Not yet.

Bolan was crouched in a window embrasure outside the dining room. Because it was a warm night, the window was open a crack. He had overheard the entire conversation.

Harry Porrelli, wearing the uniform of one of the Treynet guards, was standing with his 3-barreled gun trained at the corner of the building. The guard wasn't going to need the uniform anymore; he was wrapped up warmly in a steamer rug in the trunk of Jules Treynet's Rolls-Royce. Porrelli had not lost his expertise with the years. Most of the bleeding had been internal, and the commando knife was now back in the sheath strapped to his ankle.

He could hear music and voices from the huts on the far side of the pool. He didn't hear Bolan until the Executioner was beside him. ''The bosses are all feeding their faces in the big house,'' Bolan whispered. ''I want to get into that factory while we can. Let's go.''

Silently walking on clipped grass they skirted the graveled turnaround, past the Rolls, past the Lamborghini, a Mercedes 350 with German plates and an assortment of local sedans and pickups. Beyond a cypress hedge they could hear a chuckle of water from the pool-filtration plant. The night air was heavy with the perfume of roses.

Where every prospect pleases.... Bolan thought grimly.

The moon was high enough to cast black shadows now, transforming buildings into cardboard cutouts glittering on the surface of the water.

They kept to the shadows, stealing through a shrubbery, past the shuttered loading bays of the storage sheds, and arrived below the serrated glass roofs of the factory.

It was not very large. It didn't have to be. Sold on the open market, enough heroin to keep a man in luxury for the rest of his life would fit comfortably into a carryon airline bag, leaving room for shaving kit and pajamas. An enclosed conveyer belt, ten feet aboveground, linked factory and stores.

No windows pierced the factory walls. Spying eyes would be unwelcome at the Eagle's Nest. At the front of the building two men stood guard by a flight of steps leading to the doors. Ten feet away, an iron grill barred a truckers' delivery entrance.

Bolan looked around. The moon floated above the rim of limestone encircling the valley. Ahead, the roadway twisted down to the tunnel mouth a quarter of a mile away. Off to one side a fleet of panel trucks decorated with the Eagle Chemicals logo were parked by a gasoline pump and repair shed.

"It seems there's a bikers' rally tomorrow to help out with the distribution of the stuff," Bolan muttered. "I guess the panel trucks are used just to deliver in bulk to subcenters. After all, each biker can make personal contact with ten, twenty, thirty addicts...and no risk of discovery."

"Spooky deal." Porrelli shivered. "What's their hurry?"

"Ties in with a stepped-up terrorist campaign. I just heard them talking it over. To influence the elections. You know."

"Bastards!"

"It's up to us to make sure there's none of that shit left for them to deliver. Go do your stuff, Harry."

Porrelli tramped around the corner of the building with his weapon slung. "What the hell are you doing here?" one of the guards demanded. "We ain't relieved till midnight."

Porrelli stamped to attention in front of him. "There's been a change of plan," he announced. "J.E. wants you back at the house right now."

"What plan? What are you talkin' about? You have one hell of a funny accent, my friend. What section do you—"

The sentry never completed his question. Porrelli's blade streaked upward through the soft flesh between the two sides of the lower jawbone, slicing past the tongue to transfix the palate and sink into the brain. The man sagged, held upright only by Porrelli's grip on the hilt of the knife.

"What the hell...?" The second man started forward from the far side of the steps. Bolan jumped him from behind, a sinewy arm encircling the guy's neck before he could cry out.

He was a big man and he struggled hard. But the breath was being choked from his lungs and steely fingers exerted an agonizing, unbearable pressure on a nerve center at the side of his neck. A knee was thrust savagely into the small of his back.

For a moment the two men swayed, locked in mortal combat. The gun dropped. Desperate fingers scrabbled at Bolan's elbow. Then there was a loud snapping noise and the soldier went limp.

Bolan lowered him to the ground. Porrelli pulled the knife from his victim's throat, wiped the blade on the dead man's tunic and moved to join Bolan.

To their surprise, although no light showed, the entrance doors were unlocked. He indicated a thread of brightness below an inner door. "Working late to complete a consignment?" Bolan murmured.

The Beretta was in his hand. "Use the knife if you have to," he told Porrelli, "but don't shoot. We can't afford the sound of an unsilenced shot."

He kicked open the door. Light streamed out. Porrelli marched in.

The three white-coated men working in the neon-lit space beyond were surprised, and then reassured by the sight of the familiar uniform long enough for Bolan's eyes to accustom themselves to the dazzle and take in what there was to see.

They were standing at the entrance to a modern, expensively equipped laboratory. Fume cupboards, stainless-steel sinks and sterilizer cabinets lined the walls. Glass tubing, retorts and spiral condensers gleamed and winked on workbenches. In one corner, a centrifuge holding a dozen jars spun with a subdued hum. In another, one of the workers moved a softly flaring Bunsen burner to and fro beneath a cubicle.

Concertinaed blinds had been drawn over the slanting glass roof panels so that no light showed outside.

Chemically, the refinement of heroin is delicate and dangerous, so everything in the lab was spotless and orderly. Through an open door, Bolan saw the delivery platform stacked with sacks of raw opium, sealed packets of morphine base, hemp in bales and huge compressed blocks of cannabis resin.

The only items that looked out of place were the two Walther PPK self-loaders lying on the benches in front of the two older technicians.

Bolan downed one with a 3-burst while the guy was still picking the gun off the polished wood.

He crashed over backward onto the bench behind, dropping to the floor in a shower of spilled liquid and broken test tubes. Crimson stains spread over the front of the white lab coat as acrid fumes rose from a lifeless mouth that bubbled with acid splashed from a shattered flank.

The second man folded forward and slid to the floor with the hilt of Porrelli's expertly thrown knife protruding unicorn-style from one eye.

The technician by the Bunsen was only a boy. He had no gun. White-faced with terror, he stammered at Bolan's tall, blacksuited figure. "Don't shoot...please...I didn't..."

"All right," Bolan growled. "The guards outside this dump are changed at midnight, right? Tell me—quick—are there any routine visits, phone checks, inspections, before then?"

"N-no. Honest. None."

"How many on the strength?"

"The...strength?"

"Don't play dumb with me," Bolan rasped. "The regular guards. How many are there? Where are they now? What do they do?"

Porrelli approached the youth, his bloodied knife in one hand. "F-fi-fifty altogether," the boy cried, panicking. "Twenty on patrol, twenty on call in the barracks, the rest, well, off duty."

Porrelli fingered the point of the knife. He wiped his hand on the uniform pants he wore. "Those guys on patrol," he said. "Up on the rim. When do they come down? What are their orders?"

"They d-d-don't," the youth babbled desperately, eyeing the knife. "Not ever. Their orders are never to quit the ridge until they are relieved. Whatever happens. Mister, please don't—"

Bolan's fist traveled only a few inches but it carried all of his weight behind it. The boy crumpled and fell.

"Drag him outside," Bolan said. "In the shadow. Then fix four or five charges in this place. Pack them well in. Make sure all this slime is blown to hell." He waved an arm around the lab. "There has to be paperwork someplace. I'll take care of that."

"How much delay do you want?" Porrelli asked.

Bolan glanced at his Rolex. "It's ten-twenty now. Give us a half hour, okay? That means we have to be away to hell and gone by ten or eleven."

"Yes, sir, General," Porrelli said. He opened the pouch at his waist and limped away.

Beyond the lab, Bolan found a machine room crammed with an automated packaging plant. Here pills were bottled, powders sacheted, liquids encapsuled and various crystals shrink-wrapped in cellophane before they were put up in sacks and cartons and shipped across to the dispatch section on the conveyer belt.

Across a short corridor he found what he was looking for—the office where all the paperwork was done.

Rolling drawers out from gray metal filing cabinets, he found computer printouts listing names, addresses, incomes and political leanings of thousands of men and women likely to support the Treynet cause. Invaluable intel for any putative Fascist boss...and of course for the KGB, who would want to liquidate them once the Fascists had been betrayed.

Another section catalogued addicts who were already JETs members, together with their habits, doses and personal data. A third detailed known junkies who were not yet recruited; a fourth listed terror activities, the outrages they had committed and those planned for them in the future.

Best of all, correspondence on letterhead forged a link between Eagle Chemicals, the JETS and Schmitt-Heinkel's right-wing political party in Germany. In the hands of a responsible newspaper, that information alone would forever discredit the Treynets' claim to political credibility. No "France for the French" voters were going to support a man whose actions were governed from Germany.

In an adjoining alcove was a console, display screen and keyboard for an IBM 650 computer, along with a stack of floppy disks, several wire baskets full of rejected printouts and a FORTRAN manual.

Porrelli stood by Bolan's side. "Mission completed," he grinned.

"Great. Look, Harry, I have to photograph practically every damn document in this place. Go across the road and fix half a dozen charges in those storage sheds. Blow that filth to hell, too. Then come back here and we'll fix the computer and its data banks, okay?"

"Still thirty minutes' delay?"

"Sure. But as of now. A little less maybe, between ten-fifty and eleven. That way, the lab charges will blow first and the stores will go up later, but not so late that they can do anything about it. We can use the confusion that will result."

Bolan took the Minox from his pocket.

It was one thing to destroy the Treynets' drug stocks, wreck their evil refinery and burn their records. It was another to convince the public of the wickedness of their scheme, to blacken their reputation and ruin forever their chances of becoming a serious political force in France. For that, incontrovertible documentary proof was needed.

The Executioner would provide it.

He would deliver the spools of film to the newspaper whose columnist had been killed by the car bomb intended for Bolan himself.

He ransacked drawers, emptied files, spread papers, letters and printouts over tables, desks, the floor. He photographed everything he figured an anti-Treynet campaigner could use. He exposed six rolls of film in less than fifteen minutes.

Porrelli was back before Bolan was halfway through the final roll. "Crazy setup they got over there," he said. "I mean like they really got this thing organized! That dispatch section is something else! Sectioned by *département*, by town, by types of drug yet. They even have the crap packaged according to how strong the junkies are hooked. Can you imagine that?"

"Too bad all that organization goes up in smoke," Bolan said. "My heart bleeds for them, Harry." He wound off the last spool and put the camera away. "Okay. We've taken care of the merchandise. Now we got to see what we can do for the merchants."

IN THE MOONLIGHT the big house was a wilderness of steep roof pitches, rough-dressed stone facings and wrought ironwork. The window where Bolan had listened was one of the few not covered by slatted shutters.

Now he and Porrelli were by the door. A slender instrument from a slit pocket in Bolan's blacksuit opened the dead-bolt lock, a celluloid strip opened the Yale, and a skeleton key—the third tried from a bunch—opened the Chubb.

Inside, the hall was dark. The place smelled of furniture polish, roses and cigar smoke, with a hint of wine cookery. From the far end of the rambling building, voices—presumably the kitchen personnel—rose above the mechanized dialogue of a television drama. Porrelli went to deal with them.

Bolan stole to the only door with a crack of light showing beneath it. Judging from its position, he figured it was the entrance to the dining room. The door was heavy and thick. The tongue drew back noiselessly as he pressed down the latch. He eased the door open an inch.

It was clear at once that drama was not confined to the television screen. The tension in the softly lit room was an almost tangible thing.

Eliane Falcoz was standing. Her eyes were angry and her cheeks were red. Beside her, Jacques Edouard Treynet's handsome features were twisted into an expression of thunderstruck astonishment.

A thin, sallow-faced man on the far side of the table was speaking. "Ask her," he said viciously to Treynet. "Go on, ask her how Bolan got away from your men on the rue de Rivoli, how he made the Bois de Boulogne. The guys are wasted. They can't tell you. But I was there and I can. The bastard was given a ride in a green Lamborghini. Why don't you ask the bitch who was driving it?''

The speaker rose and pointed a quivering finger at the younger Treynet. "You think she hangs around you because she loves your beautiful mind? I tell you she's on the payroll of Interpol and she works with the Federal Narcotics Bureau. She's a common spy sent here to trap you!''

18

Mack Bolan waited outside the door, watching to see which way the ball would bounce.

If it bounced his way, he would catch it; if it bounced away, he would chase it.

He sensed the mission was entering its final phase. In principle this was how he liked to play it: a job to do with the odds stacked against him; a challenge that would tax his skills to the utmost; a gamble where there was no more planning to do, the cards already down and nothing left but action.

Greb Strakhov preferred the chess game approach, but for Bolan it was only as a poker player that he could reconcile the two disparate elements of his warrior character: the humane side with its compassion for life's civilian casualties that had earned him the title "Sergeant Mercy" in Vietnam; and the cold-blooded killing machine programmed for mortal combat with anything and everything that threatened those innocent civilians.

The second element was in command now. Bolan's nerves were as taut as a coiled spring. He was aware of the pulsing of his blood, the thumping of his heart, and he was unusually aware of the fragility of that heart, its vulnerability to the leaden death-bringers that could so soon be flying, so easily leave the lifeblood congealing on the cold floor.

There was a burst of movement in the room. Someone shouted, "Get her!" The huge Lange lunged across the table.

The Beretta in his right hand, Bolan pushed the door wide and sprang into the room.

"Okay," he yelled, "nobody move!"

Confusion.

Lange was in the center of the table amid spilled wine, broken glass and scattered flowers, his outstretched fingers grabbing for Eliane Falcoz, who had backed away with a tiny Derringer in her hand. Swanton—it had to be Swanton—was scowling at her; Strakhov's mouth was open in surprise; Jacques Edouard Treynet had jumped up, the chair lying on the floor behind him.

The elder Treynet had twisted around to face the door, eyes bulging, his cheeks mottled purple with rage.

What followed was like a remake of the holiday camp scenario...with the roles reversed.

Lange moved with incredible swiftness for a man of his bulk. Swiveling on the tabletop, he knocked over all the candles with a sweep of his legs.

The room was plunged into darkness.

The discreet thud of Bolan's Beretta was lost among the clatter of breaking dishes. He fired twice before hurling himself sideways and down, hoping to hit Lange, not daring to shoot again because now the blackness was chaotic with movement and he was afraid of winging the girl.

"Bolan!" Strakhov's voice whip-cracked in the dark. "Lange, you know what to do."

A growl of ascent told the Executioner that his shots had missed their target.

From somewhere across the room, a heavy automatic spat fire three times. Bolan heard the three slugs thunk separately into the wood of the door beside his head. He rolled sideways, gun in hand.

Eliane screamed.

A single shot from the Derringer flashed instantaneous shadows on the walls, and she screamed again.

Bolan held his flashlight now. One stab at the button and the beam lanced the dark, illuminating the standing Swanton long enough for Bolan to swing the Beretta his way and fire a single round.

The CFB agent's hands had been around the woman's throat.

The Executioner rolled again as he released the button and heard the automatic fire toward him again.

"Lights, you fools! Put on the lights. There are three of you and the man is alone."

Strakhov's furious voice came from beneath the table. Yeah, that figured. He gave the orders, others fired the guns.

The richly furnished room leaped to life. Standing by the light switch, which had illuminated a 12-lamp chandelier above the table, Jacques Edouard was pointing an automatic at Bolan. Lange was standing on the far side of the table, a Stetchkin in his vast paw.

Eliane was by the window, and Strakhov had miscounted by one. Swanton was out of the parade. He sat on the floor, red hands scrabbling at the blood pumping out through the hole in his throat. Second time around the Beretta had struck pay dirt.

"All right, Bolan," Treynet grated. "You could get one of us but not both. Throw down your gun."

At that instant the curtains billowed and the window exploded into the room in a shower of glass and Porrelli jumped through, firing his 6-shot .38-caliber Webley revolver. Behind him another man hosed lead from a Browning.

Yet again it was the titanic strength of Lange that saved the defenders. Before Porrelli's feet touched the floor he had upended the enormous table with a roar of rage.

Pandemonium.

Bottles, glasses, knives, forks and smashed dishes cascaded down along with the napkins, candlesticks and remains of the meal, leaving an oak barrier to separate Bolan, the girl and the new arrivals from the Treynet-Strakhov camp.

At the same time, Jacques Edouard extinguished the lights.

In the renewed darkness came a stamp of feet and then silence.

Bolan leaped across the room, shoes crunching on broken glass, and found the switch.

Strakhov, Lange and Treynet had vanished.

A curtain stirred between two glass-enclosed bookcases at the far end of the dining room. Behind it, a narrow door stood open.

It was only then that Bolan noticed Jules Treynet. The old man was still in his chair, his bloated face suffused dark red, his eyes wide, a victim of a fatal heart attack triggered by rage and fear.

Bolan glanced at Eliane. "You okay?"

She nodded, gasping as she massaged with one hand the scarlet weals on her neck.

"Thanks, Harry." Bolan grinned. "So who's our friend and neighbor?" He stared at the newcomer, a swarthy man with a bushy mustache.

"Search me," Porrelli replied. "What I was doing, I was trying my best to lock the goddamn kitchen staff into a pantry, and they didn't much like the idea, when along comes this guy and lends me a hand. Okay with me. He seemed wised up, and so—"

"Ancarani," the dark man said. "René Ancarani, *Direction de la Surveillance du Territoire*." The DST was the home-based section of France's counterintelligence service.

"How come you're involved in this?"

"We have been watching this Schmitt-Heinkel for some time. My superiors would be unhappy if he, or his politics, should have an undue influence in France."

"Did you know...did you know that in fact he is KGB?"

"Oh, yes," the DST agent said. "That is what *really* worries us, you see."

Before Bolan could say more, they heard Jacques Edouard Treynet's voice shouting outside the window. He was calling out the guard. In the distance an alarm bell shrilled.

Then the twelve lights danced on the chandelier and the room shook to the roar of an explosion.

The first of Porrelli's charges had blown.

19

The four remaining charges in the factory-lab exploded while Bolan and his three companions were scrambling through the shattered window. As they sprinted across the graveled turnaround and gained the shrubbery, fragments of glass and wood and cement from the pulverized walls hailed from the sky.

Jacques Edouard Treynet's voice, trembling with rage, emanated from between the parked cars and the barrack huts, distorted by a bullhorn.

"At all costs...dead or alive...a woman and three men. They *must* be caught. Every available unit. Alert the ridge guards and instruct them...on no account to escape. Is that clear? On no account..."

The words were drowned in a roar of flame; beyond the storage sheds black smoke tinged with crimson boiled up into the moonlit sky.

"So much for the computer," Bolan said with satisfaction. "Good work, Harry. In seven to ten minutes the stores go up. By then we have to be across that parade ground, among the scrub leading up to the ridge. That way, we should buy ourselves a lead on the way to the cave while they wonder what the hell's going to explode next!"

It was easier said than done. From all around them came voices and the sound of hurrying feet. Red, orange and then white floodlights appeared around the house and parade ground, exposing the property brilliantly. Sodium lamps illuminated the road to the tunnel.

Flat on their stomachs, Bolan, Porrelli, Ancarani and Eliane Falcoz crawled through the bushes toward the rear of the huts. Porrelli had recuperated his 3-barreled gun. The DST man had only his Browning automatic. One shot remained in the woman's Derringer.

Bolan handed her the Beretta and unshipped Big Thunder.

"Behind the huts on this side of the parade ground," he whispered, "there's a fifty-yard stretch of rough grass. We'll go separately. The floods are casting shadows behind the huts. Use the shadows and make a dash across the lighted strips between them, okay? Spread out. We'll rendezvous in the scrub beyond."

Treynet's amplified voice came from the other side of the pool now. Several other men shouted orders. Guards had been deployed to search the house and surrounding areas. The fugitives saw flashlight beams probing here, there. Soldiers streamed from the huts and moved toward the burning factory.

Porrelli limped behind the first hut, vanished into the shadow, then reemerged—a hurrying figure flitting over the bright strip and into the next rectangle of blackness. Ancarani followed at a touch on the shoulder from Bolan.

"What the hell happened to you at Auteuil?" Bolan asked Eliane. "I saw the Lambo on the racecourse parking lot, but no sign of you. I waited until the end of the meeting."

"I know, I saw you," she said contritely. "I'm sorry. There was no way I could tip you off. I ran into J.E., you see. He had a horse running in the third race, and of course I had to stick with him, make like I'd come specially to see his horse. When he took me back to the car and I could see you were still around, I... Well, I had to fake a sudden thirst and insist we return to the owners' tent in the paddock for another glass of champagne! I really am sorry."

"No sweat. Just so long as I know."

He focused the binoculars. Porrelli's white hair flashed into sight between the fifth and sixth huts. Ancarani was a shadow among the grasses beyond the second and third. "On your way," Bolan said. "Keep as close to the huts as you can."

When she had passed safely across the bar of moonlight between the first and second hut, he rose. Since he was the most experienced cover man, he would make the traverse farthest out of all, where the groundcover was minimal and there was the greatest chance of discovery. That way he could decoy the searchers away from the others if anyone tumbled.

Holding Big Thunder in his right hand, he parted a screen of bushes—and came face-to-face with the monolithic bulk of Lange.

Bolan was taken completely by surprise. The Russo-German giant must have been watching them, must have decided to wait until the others had gotten away so that he could take the Executioner alone, for he had been standing silent and motionless until Bolan walked into his simian arms.

Before Bolan could bring up the AutoMag, Lange struck him with the edge of his hand, temporarily paralyzing Bolan's forearm so that his fingers opened and the gun dropped.

Bolan looped in a left with all his weight, but his fist merely thudded against Lange's chest, as harmless as a child's punch. The giant moved in ponderously, reaching for Bolan.

Bolan slammed a vicious uppercut to the man's jaw; Lange shook his head, grunted, moved in still closer. Bolan jerked up his knee; Lange deflected the kick away from his groin with a meaty thigh. Bolan landed a murderous hook to the heart; Lange scarcely paused in his stride.

He was too close now to punch. His long arms seized Bolan and started to crush. Bolan struggled ferociously. Feeling was returning to his right arm but it was pinioned in

Lange's bear hug. With his left hand, with his feet, he tried every lock, every judo and karate hold that he knew.

No dice.

The KGB gorilla's grip was squeezing the breath from his lungs, making his head swim, his brain reel from lack of oxygen.

Darkness invaded his vision and the sounds of the chase floated away.

As the terrible vise grip compressed him still further, Bolan heard through increasing waves of blackness the words "I want him disabled but still conscious. Take care."

Strakhov.

Bolan squirmed feebly. The grip tightened, was released. A tremendous blow struck him in the solar plexus.

Bolan allowed himself to drop, pulling Lange down on top of him. His tortured lungs creaking as he tried desperately to suck the life-giving air back in above his savaged diaphragm, he struck and probed and gouged, using every unarmed combat trick he knew to gain time for his brain to clear, the right arm to recover, the muscles to react.

But Lange's hamlike hands were grasping his throat now, choking the remains of consciousness out of him, throttling the night away. Bolan was a swimmer going under for the third time.

Then suddenly, very loud, came a single sharp shot.

A strangled exclamation above Bolan's gagging mouth...and a slackness, an enormous weight. The grip on his throat relaxed, the hot breath wheezed from Lange's lungs.

And no more air was inhaled to replace it.

Bolan dragged himself out from under the vast body, gulping grateful lungfuls of cool air. Lange was dead, the blood between his shoulders black in the moonlight.

Eliane Falcoz stood over him, the Derringer in her hand. The second and last shot in the tiny gun had saved Bolan's life.

He struggled to his feet.

Strakhov?

Bolan was alone with the woman. They heard a receding thresh of branches among the underbrush. The spymaster knew when to concede a game.

"All I can say is thanks," Bolan panted, feeling the strength return to his limbs.

"Be my guest," said Eliane.

Shadowy in the milky light, long lines of men were strung out across the valley, beating the coverts like gamekeepers flushing birds. "Come on," Bolan said, taking the woman's arm. "We'd better make it after the others fast. That gunshot will have alerted them that there's action in this quarter."

It was true. Beyond the bushes they sensed movement all around them. Waiting to make a dash for the shadow behind the first hut they heard the sudden roar of a gunned engine and a scatter of gravel as a car turned swiftly and raced away from the house toward the road tunnel.

They could see it beneath the sodium lamps—a pale-colored Mercedes sedan with foreign plates.

Strakhov was making his exit before the pace grew too hot.

Within seconds of his departure, there were two more things to distract the pursuers' attention.

One after the other, Porrelli's charges in the storage sheds exploded. The sheds were quite small, each one perhaps the size of a four-car garage. The thudding detonations blew off the shingled roofs in a holocaust of flame, collapsed the flimsy outer walls and left flames leaping among the shattered shelves and shipping compartments of the dispatch sections inside. The aromatic odor of burning marijuana drifted through the air.

The lines of searchers wavered and broke. Nobody seemed sure now whether to seek the intruders in the shrubbery where the shot had come from, or around the buidings so systematically wrecked.

This indecision was underlined when the second event began as a distant grumble on the far side of the tunnel, swelled to a roar and finally erupted in an earsplitting reverberation that played obbligato to a firefly dance of hundreds of bright lights weaving beneath the lamps along the road to the house.

The JETs' bikers had arrived in preparation for tomorrow's rally.

In the confusion of shouted question and reply, the bellow of exhausts and the crackle of flames that still belched from the bombed lab and sheds, Bolan and his companion reached the far side of the parade ground and began climbing through the scrub toward the mouth of the cave.

The Executioner found himself next to Ancarani. "How the hell did you get in here, anyway?" he asked the DST man.

"Got myself a job," Ancarani replied. "You know. Ultraright-wing sympathizer, abolish the unions, send the Arabs back home, that sort of thing. A natural for the Treynet treatment. Until I goofed tonight, helping out your friend with the kitchen personnel, I was accepted as a fetch-and-carry stooge, a store man who could load the shit on trucks, hump bales of hemp and like that." He grinned. "Guess I'm out of a job now."

"You'd better leave with us," Bolan said. "We need your help anyway. We have to neutralize guards posted outside this cave."

The guards started firing when Bolan and his companions were fifty yards away. Flashlight beams probed as short bursts from the Uzis split the night. Two of the men were in the sandbagged emplacement—one was shouting into a radio transceiver—and the third was farther up the hillside.

Bullets thwacked through the undergrowth. Below and behind a searchlight glowed, began swinging right and left up the slope.

"We've got to grab those Uzis for ourselves," Bolan said to the DST agent. "The short-range stuff we have is no good in this kind of situation."

Ancarani made no reply.

"Porrelli and I will take them from the left," Bolan went on. "You creep up behind the sandbags and take out the one higher up. Grab the Uzi when you've zapped him and see if you can waste that searchlight down there, okay?"

Bolan paused. The bullhorn was in full cry. Across the floor of the valley, bikers were dispersing, their headlamps fingering the shadows cast by the moon.

"Ancarani?"

Still no response from the Frenchman.

Bolan stumbled, stifled an exclamation. Ancarani had already left. On his own.

Forever.

He lay on his back among the clumps of wild thyme. A stray slug had taken away half his right temple, leaving shards of skull bone white in the dark blood. His eyes were still shining but there was no life in them.

Bolan cursed. He thumbed shut the lids, checked that there were no giveaway papers on the body and joined Porrelli and Eliane farther up the hill.

The cave guards had stopped shooting. "We'll draw their fire and then home on the flashes," Bolan said. He wedged the torch in the fork of a dwarf oak and sent Porrelli and the girl out wide. When they had enough time to get in position, he pressed the button and dropped to the ground.

The beam picked out a sandbagged corner, a uniformed arm. And then flame stabbed and pulsed from the automatic weapons.

The light vanished and the torch disintegrated in a tinkle of broken glass. But a triple blast from Porrelli's Venere Extralusso and the deep-throated roar of the AutoMag punctuated the rasping chatter of the submachine guns. Porrelli followed up with six quick shots from his .38 Webley. Eliane, too, aiming the silenced Beretta above and behind the fireflashes, shot well.

There was no more shooting from the emplacement.

They scrambled up to the half-concealed cave entrance.

Porrelli wormed his way in to contact Vézoul and tell him the guards had been neutralized and it was safe to show himself.

They heard the echo of his voice. "Gilbert! Gilbert! *Nous y sommes. Tout va bien!* We made it. Everything's okay!"

As the echoes grew fainter, the sounds of pursuit grew correspondingly loud. Treynet's bullhorn was organizing the bikers and foot guards into a broad sweep advancing on the hillside. The sentry's alarm call on the radio and the shooting that followed had given them a direction. Behind the sandbags a garbled voice still quacked mechanical questions from the speaker.

Porrelli reappeared. "He's not there," he said blankly.

Bolan stared. "Not there?"

"Not a sign of him. I went in as far as I dared without a light. I called and called. Sound carries in those damned galleries. If he'd been within half a mile he'd have heard and called back."

"Should we go in and hope to meet up with him later?"

"We wouldn't have a hope in hell," Porrelli said. "Even if we still had a light."

"Maybe one of those punks carried a torch?" Bolan jerked his head at the bodies behind the sandbags.

"Look," Porrelli said, "even if he did, it's a no-way situation. Something must have happened to the old man. Without a guide you could stay down there shouting a hundred years and no one would find you. For every passageway you stumble across, there's half a dozen others look exactly the same. That's if you don't flunk out and miss an opening altogether."

Bolan bit his lip. "You mean, without him, it's out?"

"One hundred percent."

"Could we blast our way past the road tunnel?" Eliane asked.

Bolan shook his head. "No way. One guy with a submachine gun at the exit could hold up a platoon, a whole company." He looked across the slant of hillside to a dark belt of woodland. "We'll have to try the glider."

"The glider?" Porrelli repeated. "But there's three—"

"You take Eliane on the wing. I'll use that as a diversion and make it down the cliff where I killed the dogs the other day."

"We'd never make it to the top of the ridge hefting that thing."

"No, you'll have to run down toward the parade ground and the floor of the valley, hoping there's enough wind to lift you off." Bolan glanced at the sky. The breeze, which had slackened off since they quit the house, was now freshening again. Wisps of cloud drew temporary veils across the face of the moon.

"Three men and a woman…armed…dangerous. Stopped at all costs…" the bullhorn sounded from below. Some of the leading bikes were alarmingly near.

"But first we have to get there," Bolan continued. "Let's go." Running lightly among the moonlit scrub, he led the way back down to the emplacement. The two men each took an Uzi from one of the dead guards. They climbed out and continued toward the woods.

The burst of automatic fire from behind them was shockingly loud. The third guard, draped over a limestone outcrop higher up the hill, had enough life left in him to raise his submachine gun and empty the magazine.

Bolan spread the guy over the rock with a 2-shot death-blast from Big Thunder. But the lead spewed out by the Uzi had flailed across Porrelli's hips at ten yards range, almost cutting him in two.

He spun around and collapsed on his back. "Looks like you'll have to play pilot after all," he croaked.

"Enough of that," Bolan said. "We're gonna get you out of here."

"Don't make me laugh," Porrelli whispered. "It hurts when I laugh. That bastard clipped me but good. I'm through. I know it, you know it, so let's not—"

"Harry—"

"You gotta get out of here, guy. You have work to do. Me, all of a sudden I drew the wrong card. But that's the way it goes. And there's no regrets on account of—"

"We have to get out, sure. But like I said, we take you with us."

Slowly Porrelli's white head shook from side to side. "I know what I'm sayin', old buddy. It's curtains for me." The face contorted suddenly in a spasm of agony. "Finish it, soldier," he said in a stronger voice.

"Harry," Bolan said huskily, "I can't."

"You got to. There's no other way. I ain't gonna get well again, that's for sure. I'm on my way out, but they could keep me alive awhile and they could hurt me plenty. I don't want those fuckers to pull out what's left of my guts and twist them around my neck. Make it easy for me, Striker."

Red froth bubbled at Porrelli's lips. Beads of sweat on his forehead glistened in the moonlight. Below the dying man's sight, Bolan eased the muzzle of the AutoMag toward the back of his head.

Eliane was crying. She looked away. The broken body arched in another convulsion of pain. "Who needs roses?" Porrelli's voice was a rustle of dry leaves beneath the rising wind. "Make it right with the wife and kids. Tell them...sorry...but like I say, no regrets. It was...great while it lasted, Mack. Just like old times...."

"Sure," Bolan said. "Just like old times, buddy."

Yeah, the good old times when good men had to die so that bad men shouldn't make the new times worse.

Bolan gritted his teeth and pulled the trigger.

On the far side of the valley, climbing toward the wood, he saw that the pursuers had reached the sandbagged emplacement and found the dead guards. Would they figure that the fugitives had really taken to the caves? No, they had discovered the bodies of Ancarani and Porrelli. They were streaming down the slope in full cry, the bikers zigzagging with whoops and war cries, the guards firing as they came.

Two hundred yards from the wood, Bolan turned to fire a short warning burst from the Uzi and received a violent blow on the chest. The force of the impact sent him tumbling backward to crash down in among the underbrush.

He thought he had been hit, but when the girl helped him shakily to his feet he realized that although his ribs hurt like hell no bones had been broken and no blood was flowing. It was only when he felt fragments of something hard falling from his waist to his knee that he got the message.

A 9mm slug, somersaulting near the end of its trajectory, had struck the binoculars slung around his neck.

Eyepieces, prisms, lenses and frame were all shattered, but this time the field glasses had saved his life.

"A good omen…and about time," he said to the girl. "Come on. Another couple of minutes and we'll be in the air."

An overstatement.

When they reached the wing they found four bikers who had ridden up another way standing guard. Dressed in black leather studded with metal, they carried homemade burp guns. The leader was wearing a shiny black Nazi-style cap with iron crosses and a swastika armband.

"All right, buster, drop the iron," he snarled.

Mack Bolan was always ready to stand up and trade punches—or shots—with the opposition on a man to man basis. Or even when the odds were against him. Firstly because he had superb confidence in his own skill and judgment, secondly because—in the case of a shooting match— he knew how inaccurate side arms could be, especially in inexperienced hands; thirdly because, quite simply, he was a brave guy, ready to face any odds in a cause he knew to be right.

But tonight there was an extra edge to his resolution. Rage and grief had boosted him to a state that would have been reckless in another man, but in Bolan was no more than determination to ride the crest of his own personal success wave.

Without a second thought he emptied the magazine of the Uzi in a figure-eight sweep that moved down the four punks in a mess of blood and bone and ripped leather, bringing them down across the grounded bikes. The youth with the armband was the only one even to loose off a single shot, and that went high and wide.

Somewhere back in the bushes, a girl's reedy, hysterical voice screamed, "Saul! Saul!" and then broke into a fit of sobbing.

"Keep down and you won't get hurt," Bolan called. "Come this way and you follow your junkie friends, fast."

There was no more sign of life from the bushes.

He walked across to the delta wing. It was undamaged.

"It's just you and me, kid, now." He sighed. "Know how to operate one of these rigs?"

Eliane shook her head. "Negative. Just cars and power boats."

"Too bad. You'll have to ride the bike then."

"The bike?"

"Sure." Bolan pointed down the hill. The punks had ridden up a rough path that he and Porrelli had missed when they arrived. "It'll be tough. I'll perch on your shoulders. And I'll be supporting the wing. It's the only way we can be sure of making enough speed for a good lift this side of the ridge."

"You certainly do things the hard way," the girl said.

"Sometimes it's the only way."

The chase traversing the hillside from the cave mouth was no more than 250 yards away. The bike lamps bobbed among the undergrowth, sending long shadows bouncing across the slope. The mindless cries of the junkies reminded Bolan of the baying of dogs.

Real dogs were baying, too. The handlers had been called down from the rim to intercept them. A third group, gunmen from Treynet's hard-core units, were racing up from the parade ground with portable searchlights.

Bolan looked at the four bikes—a Motor Guzzi Le Mans 1000, a Suzuki GS, a big Laverda, a KZ series Kawasaki— all fast, burly machines. He decided on the Kawasaki. A trials-type wheeler stood a better chance of staying on the rough path—and there was less blood on it.

If there had not been a fallen tree near the glider they would never have made it.

As it was, two false starts frightened them before they had it right. Bolan stepped off the tree onto the pillion section of the saddle, but the wing was too unwieldy and he could not keep his balance. Eliane steered back to the trunk and he tried standing on the gas tank. That was better. He could brace his legs against her shoulders. But she was unable to control the bike.

The yelping Dobermans were very close now. The nearest bikers were fifty yards downhill. The guards were almost within range. A gust of wind moaned through the wild grasses as another cloud drifted across the moon.

"There's no other way," Bolan panted. "I'll have to sit on your shoulders, like I said. It'll be rugged because I'm no lightweight, but I'll try to keep my feet on the tank and take some of the strain off you that way. For God's sake wrap your arms around my legs and allow yourself to be lifted off the bike when I yell. Then, once we are airborne, you can climb up my body and make the second seat."

The Kawasaki stalled. Eliane kickstarted it again and wheeled it back to the tree. Bolan harnessed up and held the wing over his head. The girl sagged some beneath his weight as he transferred himself to sit astride the back of her neck. He angled his feet in and toed the tank, struggling to keep the glider's A-frame level.

She rotated the twist grip and the powerful engine roared, sending the machine and its riders careering down the path.

The bike bounced and swayed on the rough ground, lurching this way and that as Bolan, top-heavy on his precarious perch, strove desperately to stop the wing from touching the scrub on either side of the path.

They had gone no more than twenty or thirty yards when he felt the air tugging at the sail. Ten yards farther on—his arms were trembling with effort; they were hitting maybe thirty, thirty-five miles per hour—the wind gusted once more and the glider began to lift.

"That's it!" he shouted. "Let go of the bike and grab hold of me!"

He wrenched at the bar. Eliane's arms tightened around his thighs. There was a volley of shots from left, right and below. The Kawasaki fell away with its engine screaming.

Silently, with the girl dangling beneath like a circus act on a trapeze, the hang glider soared up into the sky.

20

By the time the moon appeared from behind the cloud, the hang glider was fifty feet up and banking into the wind.

The twinkling points of fire that marked the positions of the hellhounds shooting below fell away. The shattering rasp of automatic arms faded and died. Panting, Eliane hauled herself up Bolan's body and flopped into the tandem seat.

They were headed southeast toward the parade ground, the pool and the house, because the ridge was at its lowest over the road tunnel. Beyond that, the deep, wide valley of the Isère would give them a better chance for a long flight, for the opportunity to make the school at Saint Pierre where he had left the Citroën.

But first he had to coax the wing over the ridge.

Above the big house the wind suddenly dropped, and the nose of the sail dipped sharply. Floodlit below, they could see antlike figures scurrying in all directions. Then they heard the hard stammer of a machine gun, but no slugs came near.

In the dead-air zone the glider slowed almost to stalling speed; the wing's trailing edge began to flap. Bolan worked the bar like a crazy man, contriving a shallow dive that took them into the smoke column leaning over the burning storage sheds.

The smoke, still aromatic with the odor of incinerated chemicals, stung their eyes and choked them. But heat rising from the guttering fires buoyed up the delta wing, creating a thermal that sent them hundreds of feet up.

Bolan circled, seeking to gain still more height, and then glided along the valley toward the tunnel mouth.

The rock wall loomed ahead. He saw their triangular moon shadow flash upward, leaping the limestone crags, and then they hit the updraft climbing the cliff face and the wing rose again.

Skimming the crest, they passed between a lookout hut on one side and a pair of dog handlers firing useless shotguns on the other.

The distant firefly points of bikers' lamps, the blazing factory and the salvage crews trying to extinguish the flames, the house, the huts and the swarming parade ground disappeared, and the hang glider floated out over the grassy Vercors upland.

"Bravo," the girl said quietly.

Bolan managed a smile. "For what? Like the song says, a good man is hard to find, and we just lost two, maybe three. God knows what happened to Vézoul. Now there's going to be a closed dossier and a vacancy at the DST, a woman near Chambéry who will be picking roses on her lonesome, and a kid who'll have to leave school early to help out at home because his dad caught a packet fighting the fachos. You figure that for a fair bargain?"

"There are casualties in every battle," Eliane said.

"Don't tell me."

"Look at the other side of the ledger. The factory's destroyed, the stupes have gone up in smoke, they lost all their records. The photos you took will blast the drugs-and-terrorism conspiracy wide open and kill the Treynet plan forever. We have documentary evidence that will finger the hardmen and allow my drug prevention people to lean on every single addict who joined the JETs. And Jules, the old guy who was the brains behind the scheme, is dead. What more do you want, Bolan?"

"Just that...well, it would be great if we didn't have to celebrate alone," Bolan said. He sighed. "Still, I guess you're right. Right now there's no more we can do."

Wrong guess, Striker.

Several thousand feet above the moonlit floor of the Isère Valley, the sound of a nearby gunshot was so crazy, so
totally unexpected, that at first Bolan refused to believe it.

It was only when he heard a second, and a third, then saw
a segment of sky through a small rip in the sail above his
head, that he reacted instinctively and threw the glider into
a steep left turn.

But what the hell...?

Below and behind them another triangular shape stood
against the pale-lit mountain backdrop.

It was moving up on them fast. Bolan banked again as he
saw three muzzle flashes flare from beneath the sail.

They were heading into the wind. The shots were audi-
ble, but the tiny engine, downwind and with a rear air-
screw, was not.

For this one was an ultralightweight aircraft—ULW—and
the guy seated at the controls among the boxed spars beneath the A-frame was out to get them.

Jacques Edouard Treynet.

Thirsting for revenge after the wrecking of his plan, consumed with hatred for the couple who had engineered it,
maybe guessing about the film and determined at all costs
to destroy it, he had taken off after them with murder in his
heart.

Like most murderers he had the advantage over his intended victims. The machine was faster, more maneuverable than the glider. And Treynet, seated in his cage, was in
a better position to shoot than Bolan.

Newton's Law, that action and reaction are equal and
opposite, makes plenty of sense to a guy firing a gun that
recoils. He has to brace himself against that recoil in order
to keep the barrel sighted on his target. In practice, this force
is transmitted through his feet to the ground.

A man hanging in midair is less fortunate. With no solid
surface against which to brace himself, he is in effect pushed
backward with each detonation, and accuracy becomes a

matter of chance. Bolan was in the latter position now. Treynet had the ULW's cage to lean against.

Luckily for the Executioner and his passenger, the Frenchman in his fury and haste had grabbed the nearest weapon as he ran for his wing, and it happened to be a Walther PPK automatic rather than a submachine gun.

The ULW passed Bolan's delta wing fifty yards to starboard and still slightly below. "Use the Beretta. Fire at him," Bolan said urgently.

"I can't. The magazine's empty," Eliane replied.

Bolan cursed. No matter. Manipulating the control bar with his left hand, Bolan eased Big Thunder from its holster.

Treynet's ULW zoomed into a climbing turn some way ahead and then flattened out to approach them head-on and twenty feet higher up.

The pilot leaned out from his seat and emptied the PPK's magazine as he passed overhead. Three more holes appeared in the fabric of the wing. One slug struck a tubular aluminum spar and clanged away into the void.

Bolan pressed the AutoMag's trigger twice. He found that an accurate shot was impossible. The massive recoil of the big handgun swung him back in the harness and threatened to displace his hand on the bar and upset the balance of the wing.

Treynet circled and wheeled in for another pass.

Bolan dropped the glider's nose and made for the mountainside, turning into the wind and using the updraft to swing around and float higher than the ULW. He loosed off two more shots as he passed obliquely across Treynet's flight path.

For minutes the two sails banked and dived, rising, falling, turning sharply, in a grotesque parody of a World War I dogfight.

Bolan found himself outmaneuvered at every turn. The little 250cc engine, as weak as it was, gave Treynet an immense superiority in every patch of turbulence, at each thermal they encountered.

Finally the AutoMag's magazine was exhausted without a hit on the ULW as far as Bolan could see.

Seated between bracing struts, with auxiliary foot controls, Treynet could reload the Walther and had already done so twice.

Bolan carried two spare .44 clips pocketed in his black-suit, but he could not reload with one hand and he dare not let go of the bar when a false move could mean the end.

Treynet was circling closer now, looking for an opportunity to come in for the kill. He was going to approach from underneath and behind, the flyers' traditional blind spot.

Bolan handed the gun and one clip to Eliane. "Quick as you can," he urged. "The next few minutes could be rugged." And then suddenly he called out, "No, wait! Do you smoke?"

She stared at him in astonishment. "Yes. But...?"

"Got a lighter on you?"

"Yes."

"With a storm guard?"

"Why, sure. But Mack, I can't see—"

"Give it to me."

Bolan fumbled in another pocket. He had no idea why—in case they needed extra light for the photos, or to help burn the records?—but he had grabbed a few lengths of magnesium ribbon from the bench in Porrelli's workshop just before they'd left. Now he knew how he could use the stuff.

He fished out the ribbons, took the lighter and eased the wing into a long, straight glide that would allow Treynet to stalk them from behind and line up the approach he wanted.

Over his shoulder, Bolan watched the ULW overhaul his own unpowered wing. When it was within easy range for the Walther, just as Treynet raised his gun arm, he pulled the nose of the glider sharply up, so sharply that it was almost at stalling point.

Taken by surprise, Treynet sailed past beneath.

Leaning away from the wind whistling betwen the spars, Bolan flicked the lighter. The tiny flame burned brightly inside the perforated guard.

One after the other, he dipped the length of magnesium ribbon into the flame and dropped them.

The magnesium caught at once, burning up with blinding brilliance, a hot white light that seared the eyeballs.

Two of the ribbons missed their mark and flared down into the abyss beneath them. One hit Treynet's wing and then slid off into space. But the fourth caught on a projection and held fast.

The white-hot blaze burned through the sail instantly. Within tenths of a second, the material itself was aflame. As the burning edges of the hole widened, the machine lost buoyancy and began to dive.

The increased speed fanned the flames, teasing out long streamers of fire that engulfed the whole wing.

The dive became a fall.

Treynet was half standing in his seat, beating frenziedly at the blaze. They heard him screaming over the roar of the engine as he tried vainly to accelerate the ULW out of its death drop.

Bolan watched the fiery trail of smoke spiral down into the valley. The yellow flash that mushroomed out when the wreck hit the ground and the gas tank explosion were quite small.

Okay, he thought wearily. Final curtain on the Treynet scenario. Close the book. Freeze frame. End of story.

Or was it?

Sure, the mission was terminated. As ordered by Hal Brognola. Operation JETs was yesterday's smart idea. With Bolan's film, the police forces of Europe could roll up the guys still at the vacation camp and others at liberty elsewhere.

Two plans, left and right, KGB and JETs, had gone down in flames with the ULW. The Treynets were dead. Lange and Swanton were dead.

But Strakhov, the architect of the more evil plan, was still alive.

One more Hydra head had been removed, but the tentacles remained. The terrorists would scatter and reassemble someplace else. There would always be evil men to organize them. The junkies would continue to shoot. There would always be evil men to supply them.

Men like Greb Strakhov, who always escape the net.

Mack Bolan sent the delta wing soaring down the valley toward Grenoble and the morning. For him, yeah, maybe a battle had been won...but the war sure as hell was not over.

Would it ever be over?

MORE ADVENTURE NEXT MONTH WITH
MACK BOLAN

#81 Shock Waves

Crowning the capo of crime

Mack Bolan persuades a Mafia target to betray the brotherhood, as a trade for a new life in the federal witness program. But the Mob snatches the informant before he has a chance to "sing."

The trail of the traitor leads the Executioner to New York, where the local *don* is holding court to pick a Mafia monarch for the vacant throne.

Bolan crashes the coronation dinner to find the head of the snitch on the royal menu.

Enter the
'Gear Up For Adventure Sweepstakes'
You May Win a 1986 AMC Jeep® CJ
Off-road adventure — Only in a Jeep.®

OFFICIAL RULES
No Purchase Necessary

1) To enter print your name, address and zip code on an Official Entry or on a 3″ x 5″ piece of paper. Enter as often as you choose but only one entry allowed to each envelope. Entries must be postmarked by January 17, 1986 and received by January 31, 1986. Mail entries first class. In Canada to Gold Eagle Gear Up For Adventure Sweepstakes, Suite 233, 238 Davenport Rd., Toronto, Ontario M5R 1J6. In the United States to Gold Eagle® Gear Up For Adventure Sweepstakes, P.O. Box 797, Cooper Station, New York, New York 10276. Sponsor is not responsible for lost, late, misdirected or illegibile entries or mail. Sweepstakes open to residents 18 years or older at entry of Canada (except Quebec) and the United States. Employees and their immediate families and household of Harlequin Enterprises Limited, their affiliated companies, retailers, distributors, printers, agencies, \ American Motors Corporation and RONALD SMILEY INC. are excluded. This offer appears in Gold Eagle publications during the sweepstakes program and at participating retailers. All Federal, Provincial, State and local laws apply. Void in Quebec and where prohibited or restricted by law.

2) First Prize awarded is a 1986 Jeep CJ with black soft top and standard equipment. Color and delivery date subject to availability. Vehicle license, driver license, insurance, title fees and taxes are the winner's responsibility. The approximate retail value is $8,500 U.S./$10,625 Canadian. 10 Second Prizes awarded of a Sports Binocular. The approximate retail value is $90 U.S./$112.50 Canadian. 100 Third Prizes awarded of Gold Eagle Sunglasses. The approximate retail value is $6.95 U.S./$8.65 Canadian. No substitution, duplication or cash redemption of prizes. First Prize distributed from U.S.A.

3) Winners will be selected in random drawings from all valid entries under the supervision of RONALD SMILEY INC. an independent judging organization whose decisions are final. Odds of winning depend on total number of entries received. First prize winner will be notified by certified mail and must return an Affidavit of Compliance within 10 days of notification. Winner residents of Canada must correctly answer a time-related arithmetical skill-testing question. Affidavits and prizes that are refused or undeliverable will result in alternate winners randomly drawn. The First Prize winner may be asked for the use of their name and photo without additional compensation. Income tax and other taxes are prize winners' responsibility.

4) For a major prize winner list, Canadian residents send a stamped, self addressed envelope to Gold Eagle Winner Headquarters, Suite 157, 238 Davenport Road, Toronto, Ontario M5R 1J6. United States residents send a stamped, self-addressed envelope to Gold Eagle Winner Headquarters, P.O. Box 182, Bowling Green Station, New York, NY 10274. Winner list requests may not include entries and must be received by January 31, 1986 for response.

A division of
WORLDWIDE LIBRARY®

GOLD EAGLE

DON PENDLETON'S EXECUTIONER

MACK BOLAN

Sergeant Mercy in Nam…The Executioner in the Mafia Wars…Colonel John Phoenix in the Terrorist Wars…Now Mack Bolan fights his loneliest war! You've never read writing like this before. By fire and maneuver, Bolan will rack up hell in a world shock-tilted by terror. He wages unsanctioned war—everywhere!